SAFE IN PARADISE

When Zarina Bryden's parents die, she goes to live with her uncle and his wife. When he tells her she must marry the Duke of Malnesbury, a man many years her senior, Zarina is devastated. Out riding, she discovers a neighbouring estate is being sold to pay the debts run up by the owner, Darcy Linwood, who has killed himself. Rolfe, the younger brother, has come home from India to arrange the sale. Zarina has an idea. She will pay off the creditors and save the estate if Rolfe will pretend they are engaged and save her from an arranged marriage...

M

SAFE IN PARADISE

Safe In Paradise

by
Barbara Cartland

Magna Large Print Books
Long Preston, North Yorkshire,
England.

British Library Cataloguing in Publication Data.

Cartland, Barbara
  Safe in paradise.

  A catalogue record for this book is
  available from the British Library

  ISBN 0-7505-1109-5

First published in Great Britain by New English Library, 1990

Copyright © 1990 by Barbara Cartland

Cover illustration by kind permission of Rupert Crew Ltd.

Published in Large Print 1997 by arrangement with Rupert Crew Ltd.

Magna Large Print is an imprint of
Library Magna Books Ltd.
Printed and bound in Great Britain by
T.J. International Ltd., Cornwall, PL28 8RW.

AUTHOR'S NOTE

Auctions have taken place all through civilisation. There is evidence of Slave Auctions in the Homeric period of Greek history and from early Christianity to the more modern slave trade. The earliest known American Auction was held in New Amsterdam in 1662.

Over the centuries laws and regulations have been laid down in order to control fraud and abuse.

I asked the Archives Department of Coutts's Bank when cheques were first introduced, but apparently it is difficult to pin-point a specific date. The forerunners of cheques, such as 'Notes of Hand', and other 'negotiable instruments', and cheques, merged in a gradual process during the mid-18th century. The first formalised cheque-books were introduced in the 1780s.

Chapter One

1887

Zarina Bryden stepped out of the carriage which had brought her down from London and because she was excited, ran up the front steps.

The old Butler, whom she had known since she was a child, was waiting for her in the Hall. 'Welcome home, Miss Zarina,' he said. 'It warms our hearts t'have you back.'

'It is wonderful to be back, Duncan,' she replied. She talked for a few minutes, then went into the Drawing-Room.

She looked round at the familiar things she had not seen for over a year.

When her father and mother had been killed in a railway accident, she had been forced to leave home and go to London. There she had stayed with her Uncle and

Aunt. It was a sensible decision because she went to a Young Ladies' Seminary in Knightsbridge. It was a Finishing School for the daughters of Aristocrats. She made new friends.

When she came out as a Debutante she was asked to all the best parties and the most prestigious Balls.

That she had been a success was not surprising. She was not only beautiful, but also immensely rich. Colonel Harold Bryden's daughter and only child inherited his considerable fortune. She was also left an immense amount of money by her American Godmother.

When Zarina had been christened, her Godmother, who had been a friend of her mother, had come to England. Mrs Vanderstein had Russian blood somewhere in her antecedents of which she was very proud. She had insisted that her Goddaughter should be named after her. Despite the fact that she had married twice, she had no children of her own. Therefore, when she died, she had left everything she possessed to Zarina.

Society was at the moment very interested in American heiresses.

It was not surprising therefore, that Zarina, with such a bank balance, should attract a great deal of attention. There was no doubt that she was a beauty. Young men who had begged her to become their wives were not entirely influenced by the mountain of dollars that she possessed.

Now that the Season was over Zarina had been determined to return to her house in the country. To her it had been and always would be—home. She had suggested returning before now, but her Uncle and Aunt had thought it a mistake to revive the misery she had felt when she lost her father and mother.

Now, looking round the Drawing-Room, it swept over her how much Bryden Hall meant to her. She could see her mother sitting in a chair by the window. It was where she sat when she read Zarina the Fairy Stories she had loved when she was small.

It was through her father that she had enjoyed the books that filled the

Library. There he had described to her the many countries he had visited, and how fascinating they were. 'As soon as you are older, my Poppet,' he said, 'I will take you to Egypt to see the Pyramids and we will pass through the Suez Canal that was only opened eighteen years ago, and on through the Red Sea.'

'Oh, let us go now, Papa,' Zarina had begged.

He had shaken his head. 'There is a great deal more for you to learn at home before you start exploring the world. As I have told you so often, I like women who are intelligent like your mother, and not empty-headed, like so many Socialites.' Zarina remembered how scathing he had been about the many Beauties who were such a success in London.

She had learnt, when she moved into the Social Scene, that they were pursued by the Prince of Wales. She had of course seen His Royal Highness looking exceedingly smart and very dashing. Her contemporaries quickly told her that he was not interested in girls and she would never be invited to Marlborough House. It had not troubled her in the slightest. But she realised that her Aunt Edith would have enjoyed every minute of being in the 'Royal presence'.

Lady Bryden, however, knew quite a number of distinguished hostesses. Zarina's Uncle, General Sir Alexander Bryden, had commanded the Household Cavalry, which made him *persona grata* in most Social circles. Zarina found him awe-inspiring. Yet, as he was her Guardian, she realised that if she was to do what she wanted, she had to gain his approval. It had been hard work to persuade him that as soon as the Season was over she could go home.

'Your Aunt has a great many things to do in London,' he said.

'Then I tell you what, Uncle Alexander,' she said, 'you and I could go down to Bryden Hall for a few days. I must see what is happening there and, after all, now that Papa is dead the people in the village as well as those who work on the Estate are *my* people.'

She made it sound as if it was her duty,

13

knowing that was something her Uncle would understand.

He therefore capitulated, saying: 'Very well, Zarina, we will go down on Thursday and perhaps stay a week. I will try to persuade your Aunt to join us, but I know she has several Committee Meetings she must attend.'

Lady Bryden was very given to 'good works', especially since it brought her into contact with some of the most distinguished Peeresses and minor Royals.

Looking round the Drawing-Room, Zarina felt her mother's presence so strongly that it was almost as if she could talk to her. She had known she would feel like this when she came home and she had no wish to avoid it. She jumped when she heard Duncan's voice say: 'I thinks, Miss Zarina, you'd like your tea served in th' Library, like you used to in th' old days.'

'Of course I would, Duncan,' Zarina replied. 'It is very kind of you to think of it.'

She pulled off her hat and travelling cloak and handed them to him. 'My

14

Lady's-Maid is travelling in the Brake with the General's Valet. I expect Mrs Merryweather will show her round.'

'She's waiting t' do that, Miss Zarina,' Duncan replied, 'and longing t' see you, just as is Cook and o' course Jenkins in th' stables.'

'I want to see everybody and everything!' Zarina smiled. 'Oh, Duncan, it is wonderful to be home! I have missed you all, just as I miss..Papa and..Mama.' The tears came into her eyes as she spoke of them.

Duncan, as he had done when she was a child, patted her on the shoulder and said: 'Now, don't you upset yourself, Miss Zarina. The Master'd want you t' be brave, an' there's a great many things for you t' do now that you've come home.'

Zarina wiped away her tears.

They walked along the passage which led to the Library. It was a beautiful room with a brass balcony along one wall which was reached by a ladder of twisting wooden steps. Zarina had loved to climb up it when she was a child. She thought that when she was alone she would climb them again.

15

Tea was arranged in front of the fireplace. Because it was Summer, instead of a fire, flowers filled the hearth.

'I wonders how long th' General'll be, Miss Zarina?' Duncan asked. 'If he's not far behind I'll go and fetch another cup.'

'He is travelling by train, and should be here at half past six, in time for dinner,' Zarina replied. 'Tell Jenkins to meet him at the Station.'

'Very good, Miss Zarina,' Duncan answered, 'an' will Her Ladyship be accompanying him?'

'No. My Aunt had to stay in London,' Zarina explained.

She smiled at the old man as she said: 'I would really prefer to be here on my own. I am sure Jenkins has kept the horses well exercised for me.'

'That he has, Miss Zarina! he's been a-grooming 'em 'til their coats shine like satin!'

Zarina laughed. She understood quite well that everything had been done to make her homecoming a happy one.

Although she had been in London, she

16

had kept in touch with Mr Bennett, who was in charge of the house and the Estate. Her father had trusted him and she knew she could do the same. He had written every week to tell her what was happening in the village and amongst her own people. She wrote letters of congratulation to those who had a Golden Wedding and there were presents for any villagers who were married. She also sent congratulations to those who had a baby. She had instructed Mr Bennett to put up the wages of those who worked for her. She could afford it and she wanted the Estate to look as good as her father had made it, possibly even better.

Now as she sat down to drink her tea, she asked Duncan questions about the people she remembered.

The Vicar had always been a favourite ever since he had prepared her for her Confirmation.

'The Reverend's just th' same,' Duncan told her, 'he's got a bit older an' his hair's turning grey, but he be as kind as he always were.' He paused before he added: 'He's having a bit of trouble wi' his son, but I 'spect Mr Bennett'll tell you about that.'

'I know Mr Walter had three different jobs last year,' Zarina answered. 'Surely, he has settled down by now?'

Duncan shook his head. 'One can never be sure wi' Mr Walter.'

They talked about the Vicar's family for a short while, then Zarina enquired about the Doctor and his children and the people who kept the shop. She was relieved to hear they were all there and there were few changes.

By this time she had finished her tea. Leaving Duncan to clear away she went upstairs. She could hear her Lady's-Maid and Mrs Merryweather talking in her bedroom.

She passed the half-open door and went to the Master Suite. It was where her father and mother had always slept.

She opened the door and was instantly aware of the scent of *pot-pourri* and lavender. Once again she felt as if her parents were there, waiting for her.

The curtains were closed over the windows and she drew them back to let in the sunshine. She looked at the big four-poster bed. How often she had climbed into it to lie beside her mother and beg for a story.

It was an agony to come back and not find them there; yet it was something she had to do. She felt that for too long she had neglected the people she employed and who loved her because she was her father's daughter.

'Whatever Uncle Alexander and Aunt Edith say,' she told herself, 'I am going to stay here at least during the Autumn.'

It had been exciting to be in London, she would not deny that. It was also a thrill to find she was such a success. At the same time, it was impossible not to know when she entered a Ball-Room that the Dowagers were murmuring to each other: '*That* is the Heiress.'

The same thing occurred when she appeared at a party, a luncheon, or a Reception.

At first it made her feel self-conscious,

then, while she tried to ignore it, she could not help being aware that her money labelled her. There was no escape from it. Because she was intelligent she told herself that it must not be a barrier between her and other people. Yet she was on guard when a young man led her out into the garden and without any prevarication said: 'I love you, Zarina, and I want more than I have ever wanted anything in my life, to make you my wife.'

It sounded so sincere.

There was no doubt that he *looked* as if he was in love.

At the same time, Zarina had been told that the man in question was heavily in debt. Or else he was the son of a distinguished Aristocrat whose older brother would inherit everything.

What was more, she was suspicious, although she tried not to be, of any proposal which came, she thought, on too brief an acquaintance. What was the hurry—unless the man in question wanted her money?

Why could he not wait and become

friends? He could then discover if they were really in love with each other.

There was only one answer to that.

The over-eager suitors were afraid some other man would get there before them. 'Getting there' meant having control of her money.

'Supposing I was penniless?' she asked one night. 'I wonder what would have happened then?'

She had just returned from a Ball, having received three proposals of marriage. She knew the truth, and it was very humiliating.

Now, she told herself as she opened a window in her mother and father's bedroom, she was home. The people here had loved her before she was rich. They would not love her any more because she had so many American dollars in the Bank.

She looked out over the garden with its smooth green lawns and colourful flower-beds. Beyond them were the trees which she had climbed as soon as she was old enough to do so.

'I love it! I love every blade of grass, every bird in the trees and every bee buzzing over the flowers,' she thought. 'I am home, home! And no one shall spoil it for me!'

She stayed for a long time in her parents' room, then she went in the *Boudoir* next door which contained many of her mother's treasures. There were china ornaments about which she had told Zarina stories; pictures on the walls that her father had given his wife because she loved French artists. There were special books which her mother read again and again because she said they inspired her.

'I shall read them as I have read them before,' Zarina promised herself.

It was some time later that she heard a carriage draw up outside and knew that her Uncle had arrived. She wished he had not come and she could be alone. When she had suggested there was no reason to take him away from London her Aunt had been horrified.

'Of course you must be Chaperoned,' she said.

'Surely not when I am staying in my own home?' Zarina replied.

'You are not a child with a Nurse in charge of you,' her Aunt Edith said sharply. 'You are a young woman. If a gentleman called on you when you had no Chaperone it would be very improper for you even to speak to him!'

There was no use arguing and Zarina had accepted the inevitable.

Now her Uncle had arrived.

She thought he would somehow spoil the atmosphere of the house and her joy at being home.

As she walked along the corridor towards her own bedroom she could hear his voice, strong and dominant, in the hall. She went into her bedroom, found Mrs Merryweather there and kissed her affectionately.

'It's a real joy to see you, Miss Zarina!' Mrs Merryweather exclaimed.

'It is wonderful to be home,' Zarina answered, 'and it is looking as perfect as it always was. I am so grateful to you.'

'We've done our best,' Mrs Merry-weather said with obvious satisfaction. 'It'll be just like old times to have you with us.'

Zarina had a bath which the Housemaids placed in front of the fireplace. Hot water in polished brass cans was carried up by two footmen. She pretended she was not grown up, but still a child. She expected to hear her Nanny say: 'Come along, slow-coach. It's time for bed!'

Instead she put on one of her pretty, expensive gowns, which her Aunt had chosen for her in Bond Street and went downstairs.

She had only been in the Drawing-Room for a few minutes before her Uncle appeared. He was looking very smart in his evening clothes. His grey hair, which was growing a little thin, was brushed back meticulously. Everything about him was, in the words of his Valet 'spick and span'. Zarina knew it was what he expected of the troops he commanded.

'Here I am, Zarina!' the General said as he walked towards her. 'The train was late—as might be expected!'

'It is nice to see you, Uncle Alexander,' Zarina said, kissing his cheek. 'Duncan has opened a bottle of champagne to celebrate my return home.'

'Champagne, eh?' the General exclaimed. 'Well, I will not say "No", after what has been an uncomfortable and tiring journey. People go into ecstasies about the convenience of the railways, but I prefer my horses.'

'I feel the same,' Zarina smiled. 'It only took us just over three hours to get here, and it was lovely travelling through the countryside.'

They talked about the Estate when they were at dinner and the General said: 'We will look at the farms tomorrow and see what progress has been made in clearing the trees in the woods which were felled during the storms last Winter.'

'I am sure we will find everything exactly as we want it,' Zarina said. 'Mr Bennett is very efficient.'

'It is always a mistake not to inspect everything one owns down to the last stone,' the General said. 'And that is what we must do, my dear, before we go back to London.'

There was a little pause before Zarina said: 'I was just thinking, Uncle Alexander, that I would like to stay on here, at least until the Winter. After all, it is my home, and if you and Aunt Edith insist on my having a Chaperone, perhaps one of my old Governesses would come to stay with me.'

The General did not speak for a moment. He drank a little of the claret which Duncan had poured out for him before he said: 'That is something, my dear, I wish to talk to you about—after dinner.' The way he spoke made it clear to Zarina that it was a subject he did not wish to discuss in front of the servants. She wondered what he was going to say.

While they talked of other things, she told herself she would not be dissuaded from doing what she wanted. And what she wanted was to stay in her own home. At any rate, there were at least two months before what was thought of as the 'Winter

Season' started. That would not be until the Queen returned from Balmoral. The majority of the men who had been shooting grouse in Scotland would also return to London.

'I would rather ride my horses over my own land than go trit-trotting in Rotten Row!' Zarina thought. She had the feeling, however, that her Uncle was going to oppose any suggestion she might make.

He would expect her to obey him.

'I will not do it,' she told herself indignantly. 'He may be my Guardian, but it is *my* money I am spending and I am entitled to have a will of my own.'

She was however apprehensive.

After they had finished the coffee and the General had drunk a small glass of Port, they left the Dining-Room. He had already said he had no wish for her to leave him as would have been correct. The way he spoke made Zarina wonder if he was suspicious that she might disappear by going up to bed.

'I really am rather tired,' she told herself as they went into the Drawing-Room. 'I do not want any disagreeableness with Uncle Alexander on my first night at home.'

Duncan had lit the crystal chandeliers which made the whole room look lovely. If only, Zarina thought, her father and mother were waiting for her, how happy they would all be. She remembered how her father would laugh at many things she said. Her mother would look at her with love in her eyes and she knew how much she meant to them both.

The General went to stand in front of the fireplace. Zarina was aware by the expression on his face that he was going to give her a lecture of some sort. She tried to remember if she had done anything wrong, but could think of nothing.

Because he expected it she sat down on a sofa just a little way from him. She put her hands demurely in her lap.

'One of the reasons why I did not accompany you, Zarina, when you left,' the General began, 'was because I had a very important interview which concerns you and your future.'

28

'Concerns me, Uncle Alexander?' Zarina exclaimed.

It flashed through her mind that he must have been approached by one of the men who had proposed to her the previous night at a Ball given by the Duchess of Devonshire. It had been a very impressive occasion. Her Aunt had been delighted when she had received the invitation. Devonshire House was in Piccadilly. With its gold-tipped railings and its garden which swept down towards Berkeley Square it was one of the most outstanding houses in London. So were its owners. The Duchess, who had previously been the wife of the Duke of Manchester, was a great beauty. Now, when she entertained as the Duchess of Devonshire, nobody refused her invitations. 'You will enjoy every minute of it,' Lady Bryden had said to Zarina excitedly when the invitation arrived, 'and of course you must have a new gown, even though there are still two in your wardrobe you have not yet worn.'

Zarina thought it was a needless extravagance. Although money was no object, she grudged the time it took fitting the gown when she might have been riding or driving in the Park. However, to please her Aunt, she had gone to the most expensive shop in Bond Street. The gown was certainly the most beautiful she had ever owned. It was, of course, white—no debutante would dare wear a 'colour'. It was embroidered with pearls and diamante and it showed off her exceedingly small waist. It was also a perfect foil for her fair hair with touches of gold in it, and the whiteness of her skin.

When she arrived at the Ball with her Aunt, glittering with diamonds, she was not surprised that they caused a sensation, despite the fact that the room was filled with people of far greater Social importance than themselves.

Zarina was besieged by partners. Before she left in the early hours of the morning, she had received two proposals of marriage. She found it difficult to say 'no', and even more difficult to escape from their persistence, therefore she had learnt to reply that they must 'speak' to her Uncle. She had found this very effective as the General could be awe-inspiring and overpowering.

One young man after another had left his house in Belgrave Square with what her Uncle described as 'Their tails between their legs'.

'I know all about that young whipper-snapper who came to see me this morning,' he would say to Zarina. 'Up to his neck in debt and a family history I would not wish on my worst enemy.'

'Thank you, Uncle Alexander, for dealing with him,' Zarina replied. 'It is difficult for me to make them understand that I have no wish to marry anyone.'

'You did exactly the right thing in sending him to me,' the General approved.

Zarina thought he was, in fact, an excellent 'watch-dog'! Sir Alexander actually would not have deemed the description a compliment.

Now, she thought as neither of the two men who had proposed were desirable, she had no wish to see them again.

'You may be surprised to learn,' the General was saying, 'that my visitor, who called about half-an-hour after you left,

31

was the Duke of Malnesbury.'

Zarina wondered how this could concern her.

'I have known him for many years,' the General went on. 'In fact we served in the same Regiment together before he succeeded. When he asked me to receive him, however, I did not realise the reason for his request.'

Zarina, listening, thought her Uncle was taking a long time in getting to the point. She could still see no reason why the Duke should in any way, concern her.

'What Malnesbury came to ask me,' the General said slowly, as if he were considering every word, 'quite correctly, and it is certainly an example to many younger men, was if he could be permitted to pay his addresses to you.'

Zarina stared at her Uncle in astonishment. 'Pay..his addresses?' she repeated. 'What did he mean by that?'

'It means, my dear, as you should be aware, that you have received the great honour of His Grace wishing you to be his wife.'

For a moment Zarina was speechless. Then after a moment she said: 'His..wife? But..he is..very old!'

'Malnesbury must be a little over fifty-five,' the General replied, 'but he is in good health, an athletic man who spends most of his time in the country.'

'I remember talking to him at Lady Coventry's party last Wednesday,' Zarina said. 'I think I danced with him at a very boring Ball we went to in Grosvenor Square, but otherwise, I have never spoken to him.' She laughed. 'I only hope you told him that the whole idea was impossible.'

'Impossible?' the General exclaimed. 'Do you know what you are saying?'

'Of course I do,' Zarina replied, 'and between you and me, Uncle, I think it is rather a cheek for a man of that age who is almost old enough to be my grandfather, to suggest anything so ridiculous.'

'You do not know what you are saying,' the General said sharply. 'Malnesbury may not be a young boy. At the same time, he has been a widower for five years and he has no heir.' He paused to scowl at her before he continued: 'In fact, I think I am right in saying he has five or six daughters, but no son.'

'I am not concerned with what he has or has not,' Zarina said, 'and if you try to encourage him, Uncle Alexander, it will be a great mistake. I would not marry the Duke if he was the last man on earth!'

'Good God, girl! Are you crazy?' the General asked angrily. 'Most young women would jump at the chance of the Duke of Malnesbury so much as *looking* at them.' He almost stumbled over the words as he went on: 'He wants you to be his *wife!* His *wife*—you stupid little fool. That means you will be a Duchess and have a traditional post as Lady-of-the-Bedchamber to Her Majesty.'

Zarina clenched her fingers together.

'All I can say, Uncle Alexander, is that if you encourage the Duke to think I might consider him as my husband you are making a great mistake. As I have already said, I would not marry him if he was the last man in the world!'

'That is where you are mistaken—very mistaken!' the General said slowly. 'I have told the Duke I welcome his suggestion and that he will not only pay his addresses to you, but that I accept him wholeheartedly as your future husband.'

Zarina drew in her breath. She knew from the way her Uncle was speaking that he was forcing his will upon her. She knew she would have to fight him to save herself.

'You may find it..difficult to..understand this,' she said, 'but I have no..wish to be a Duchess, or in fact to marry..any man I do not..love. How could I possibly love somebody like..the Duke who is..old enough to be my..grandfather?'

'That is an idiotic remark and untrue,' the General started to say.

'Idiotic, or not,' Zarina interrupted, 'I will not marry him and if you have accepted him as a suitor you will just have to tell him that you made a mistake.'

There was silence for a moment. Then the General said in a voice he might have used to a recalcitrant raw recruit: 'You will obey me because you have no choice in the matter!'

'What can you mean by that?' Zarina enquired.

'I mean that you are my Ward and, until you are twenty-one, you must obey me because that is the law of the land.'

'You cannot force me to marry someone I do not wish to marry!'

'You will marry him,' the General said, 'if I have to drag you up the aisle to make you do so!'

Suddenly the General's voice changed and he said angrily: 'Who the hell do you think you are that you can refuse a man as important as the Duke? You may have money, and I am not saying that the Duke would not find that a welcome asset. At the same time, he has fallen in love with you, you stupid little idiot!' He glared at her before continuing: 'He was ecstatic over your beauty and your charm! Listening, I could only think there was no young woman more fortunate than you in the whole country!'

'Fortunate!' Zarina cried. 'Being married

to an old man I do not love when I can have the choice of any number of young, delightful, charming men?'

'Who have they been so far?' the General asked. 'A lot of "ne'er-do-wells" who have nothing to offer you except a collection of debts.'

'That is not entirely true,' Zarina protested. 'When I marry it will be to a man I love and who loves me for myself.'

The General gave an ugly laugh. 'Do you think it possible with all your money that any man will want you entirely for yourself? If so, you are living in a dream world. Most men are practical. They marry for blue-blood, property, or for money.' He paused before he went on: 'You have the latter, and although you come from a decent, respectable County family, you can hardly pretend you are the equal of the Duke of Malnesbury.' He drew in his breath and continued: 'What you have to do is to go down on your knees and thank God that anyone so distinguished and so important should want you as a woman.'

'Whatever you may..say I will not..marry him!' Zarina argued. She was very pale and, because her Uncle frightened her, her hands were trembling. At the same time, she was determined she would not give in to him.

'You can talk and talk,' she said, 'but I will not listen to you. Let me tell you now, and for the last time, that I will..not marry..the Duke.'

'If you think you can defy me, you are very much mistaken,' the General said angrily. 'Because you were an only child you have been spoilt and it is about time you were beaten into submission.' He had an expression of rage as he went on: 'I am not speaking lightly when I tell you that is what I shall do if you try to disobey me. By the time we return to London you will realise I am doing what is best for you and best for the family. I will have no argument about it. You *will* marry Malnesbury.'

'I will not marry him..I will not!' Zarina replied. She jumped up from the sofa. Because her Uncle looked so menacing and she thought he might hit her, she ran to the door. She pulled it open, then she looked back to see that he had not moved, as she was afraid he might have done.

'I hate..you!' she said, 'and if Papa was alive he would not..let you bully me!'

With these last words she went out of the room and slammed the door behind her. Then she was running up the stairs to her bedroom as if it was the one sanctuary to which she could escape.

Chapter Two

Zarina tossed and turned all night. It was impossible to sleep. All she could think of was the Duke menacing her, old and grey, slow, boring and to her, repulsive.

By the morning she felt as if she was becoming hysterical. She knew the only way she could feel calmer was to go riding. She got up before her maid came to call her and dressed herself. Then she went down a secondary staircase so that the Housemaids who were working in the hall, would not see her.

She had almost reached the bottom of the staircase when she saw Mr Bennett come in from a side door and go into his office. She was looking forward to seeing him, yet at this moment she did not wish to talk to anyone. Also, she had no wish to be greeted enthusiastically with how well the Estate was doing. If her Uncle had his way she would be whisked away to live in the Ducal Castle in Lincolnshire.

She heard Mr Bennett close the door of his office and slipped past and out through the door by which he had just entered.

It was only a short way to the stables. There she found, as she expected, Jenkins, who had looked after her father's horses ever since she could remember.

When he saw her he held out his hand and said: 'How are ye, Miss Zarina? 'Tis too long since ye've bin ridin' th' horses.'

'I know that, Jenkins,' Zarina replied. 'It is something to which I have greatly been looking forward. How are they all?'

'Now, ye come an' have a look at 'em,'

Jenkins said proudly.

She went into the stables and started to go from stall to stall. The horses were certainly in good shape. She knew there was no one better as a Head Groom than Jenkins. Finally she said: 'Saddle *Kingfisher* for me. I want to ride all over my favourite fields.'

'Oi thought that's wot ye'd say, Miss Zarina,' Jenkins said in a tone of satisfaction.

He fetched a bridle and girth for *Kingfisher*, and, as he was putting them on, he said: 'Don't ye go ridin' near t'Priory t'day, Miss Zarina. It'd only upset ye.'

'Upset me?' Zarina exclaimed. 'Why should it do that?'

Jenkins fastened the bridle and girth before he said: 'There be th' Auction Sale takin' place there t'day.'

'A Sale?' Zarina said. 'What Sale?' What are you talking about?'

Jenkins looked at her in surprise. 'D'ye mean ye've not 'eard wot's 'appened?'

'I have heard nothing, and Mr Bennett did not mention the Priory in his letters.'

41

She thought as she spoke that Bennett's letters had been strictly about her own Estate, the house and the village. The Priory, which belonged to the Earl of Linwood, was about two miles away across the fields. The estate marched with her father's.

'It be a sad story,' Jenkins was saying. 'If 'e knowed wot was 'appenin', 'Is late Lordship'd turn in his grave, he would!'

'What *is* happening?' Zarina persisted.

'Well, 'Is Lordship be in bad health,' Jenkins began, 'an' Mr Darcy, as us allus called him, were gettin' into trouble in London.'

Zarina, of course, remembered the Viscount Lin. The old people on the Estate always called him 'Master Darcy', when she was a small girl, just as they called his brother 'Master Rolfe'. Both boys were several years older than her, but, as her father and mother were close friends with the Earl, she often met them.

'What has happened to Mr Darcy?' she asked now.

'We all knowed as he were up t'some

mischief or other,' Jenkins answered, 'an' when he come home, his Lordship an' he would have high words 'bout it.'

Zarina understood. Darcy had been exceedingly good-looking. Even when he was a teenager she had heard her Nurse and her Governesses talking about his extravagance and his love-affairs.

'It all comes to a head 'bout two months ago,' Jenkins continued. 'No one knows 'xactly wot happened, 'cept it were whispered as Mr Darcy was being threatened wi' bein' took to prison.'

'To prison?' Zarina exclaimed. 'But, surely, that did not happen?'

'Oi thinks meself t'would have,' Jenkins replied, 'if he'd not had wot t'said in the newspapers were an accident wi' his gun.'

Zarina stared at him. Then she asked in a whisper: 'Are you saying that Mr Darcy shot himself?'

Jenkins nodded. 'That's wot they all thinks he did, an' it killed His Lordship. He 'as a stroke when he hears th' news, an' he never recovered. Th' Doctors couldn't do nothin' fer him.'

'How terrible!' Zarina exclaimed. 'I had no idea of this happening.'

'T'were in t'newspapers,' Jenkins said.

Zarina felt guilty. While she had been enjoying so many engagements she had not read *The Times* or the *Morning Post* very carefully although they were always in her Uncle's Study. She thought now that the General had undoubtedly known about it, but had kept it from her. He might have thought it would upset her that one of her father's oldest friends had died. She said reflectively: 'You said just now there is to be a Sale.'

'Mr Rolfe's back from somewhere in th' East, where he were when 'Is Lordship died. Oi understands from wot they tells me, to meet Mr Darcy's debts he be sellin' everythin', an' th' Priory itself.'

'I do not believe it!' Zarina exclaimed. 'How can he sell the Priory? It has been in the Linwood family centuries.'

'You be roight,' Jenkins said, 'an' o' course, we're all a-wonderin' who'll buy it an' wot'll happen to them as have worked

44

in t'house and on th' Estate, an' if they'll be told t'go.'

Zarina knew only too well how disastrous this would be. Most of those who worked on the Linwood Estate, like those on hers, had followed in the footsteps of their father, their grandfathers and their great grandfathers.

The Priory itself was one of the most beautiful houses she had ever seen. It had come into the possession of the first Earl of Linwood on the Dissolution of the Monasteries. It had been given him by Henry VIII for deeds of gallantry he had performed whilst serving the King.

'How can Rolfe let it go in that callous manner?' she asked herself.

'Th' 'le thing be a bombshell,' Jenkins said, 'an' Oi'd no wish, Miss Zarina, to upset ye th' first day yer come home.' He stopped a moment and then went on: 'But, as t'Sale be taken' place at two o'clock, there'll be crowds goin' to see who buys th' furniture an' th' pictures. But wot really concerns 'em is who'll be buying th' Priory.'

Zarina did not reply. She was thinking of how tragic it was and how upset her father and mother would have been. They would have tried to help the Earl where Darcy was concerned, if they had been alive.

She was quite certain, too, that they would have helped Rolfe. He was having to part with his home and everything that he had loved ever since he was a boy.

She could remember the first children's party to which she had been taken at the Priory. She had been very small at the time, and had been carried about by her Nurse. The boys had played *Musical Chairs* and *Oranges and Lemons* with other children of their own age. Later, when she was older they would tease her but then they would pick her up in their arms so that she could take one of the best presents off the Christmas Tree.

The Priory had always fascinated her. There was a huge Banqueting Hall where the monks had sat at long refectory tables. Then there was the Chapel which was exceedingly beautiful. The rooms decorated by the Countess, had seemed in some way magical.

'Oi sez to th' wife on'y yesterday,' Jenkins was saying as he fastened the girths under *Kingfisher*, 'that th' Colonel would've bin reel upset, he would, if he knowed wot was a-goin' on.'

'I am sure Papa would have tried to help Mr Rolfe now,' Zarina murmured.

Suddenly she told herself that was what she must do. Of course she could help—who could afford it better? The idea seemed to flash through her mind like a streak of lightning.

Jenkins had finished saddling *Kingfisher*. He was just about to take him out of his stall when Zarina said: 'Wait a minute. Saddle a horse for Mr Bennett. I am just going back to the house to speak to him.'

She did not wait for Jenkins to reply but she ran across the cobbled yard and back through the side door into the house. She opened the door of Mr Bennett's office and found him, as she expected, sitting at his desk. He rose as soon as he saw her and

47

with a smile held out his hand. 'Welcome home, Miss Zarina!' he said. 'You have been away for too long.'

'That is what I feel,' Zarina said. 'Now, Mr Bennett, before we say any more, I want you to come with me to the Priory.'

'The Priory,' Mr Bennett exclaimed. 'I am sorry you should hear about that as soon as you have returned.'

'Jenkins has been telling me what has happened,' Zarina said. Furtively she glanced over her shoulder. 'I want you to come with me now,' she said in a low voice, 'and bring your cheque books with you.'

'But, Miss Zarina..' Mr Bennett began.

Zarina held up her hand. 'You must come at once,' she said. 'We will talk on the way.'

She felt it was imperative for them to leave immediately. If her Uncle, who was an early riser, chose to come downstairs, he might enquire where she was going. He would then, she was sure, try to prevent her from visiting the Priory.

Now she thought about it, she was certain that he must have known what had happened to the Earl, and to Darcy. He had deliberately kept the news from her because he had not wanted her to worry about what was happening at home when she was such a success in London.

'It was wrong of him not to tell me,' she thought, and was determined he should not interfere now.

'Come quickly!' she said, 'and, as I have already said, bring my cheque-book!'

On the General's advice, she had given Power of Attorney to Mr Bennett where the house and the Estate were concerned. Although a minor, she had complete control of her money.

'I want you to enjoy yourself, my dear,' he had said to Zarina. 'It would be very irksome to have to continually write cheques for rates, or be consulted about the cost of repairs. You can trust Bennett.'

'I know that,' Zarina replied. 'Papa found him excellent in every way.'

She had therefore done as her Uncle suggested. She wrote to Coutts Bank instructing them to honour any cheques that were signed by William Bennett.

She had not thought about it again.

Now she was aware that Mr Bennett was very surprised at what she was asking of him. However, he obeyed her without any prevarication. As he took the cheque-book from a drawer of his desk, Zarina walked from the room.

By the time she reached the Stable-Yard Jenkins had both horses waiting for her. *Kingfisher* was beside the mounting-block.

Mr Bennett had ridden to his office from his house which was at the far end of the drive. He was therefore wearing riding-boots. As he joined Zarina he was carrying his crop in his hand.

Without speaking, she moved towards the other end of the Yard beyond which were the Paddocks. Then there was some flat land on which she had always galloped with her father. Mr Bennett caught up with her as she reached them. She thought with satisfaction that, at least for the moment, she had escaped from the General.

Because she wished to put a considerable

distance between her Uncle and herself she still rode swiftly. She turned into one of the woods which divided the two Estates.

There was a broad drive through the centre.

As their horses slowed down, Zarina said to Mr Bennett: 'I have an idea of what I am going to do when I reach the Priory, but I do not want to talk about it until I have discussed the situation with Mr Rolfe. I suppose I should say, His Lordship.'

'I understand,' Mr Bennett replied. 'At the same time, if you will forgive me saying so, before you do anything hasty, you should talk it over with the General.'

'That is something I have no intention of doing,' Zarina said in a hard voice. 'I am now grown up and I wish to decide my own life, specially anything which concerns my happiness.'

Mr Bennett gave her a quick glance and she knew he was curious but she had no intention of saying any more, and merely rode on as quickly as she could.

It took them only a little over half an hour to come in sight of the Priory. The

Monks who had built it had chosen a perfect site. The piece of raised land had a wood behind it to protect the building from the winter winds. As was traditional, it was a long building of white stone and it gleamed like a gem against a green velvet background. In front was a stream in which the monks had fished. It was there that Darcy and Rolfe had rowed small boats and swum in the summer.

The nearer Zarina got to it, the more beautiful it looked. 'How can he bear to part with anything which is so perfect,' she asked herself.

Now, as they drew a little nearer, they saw there was a number of carriages parked in the Court-Yard at the front of the house. Nearer still they saw a crowd of people on foot approaching up the long drive.

Zarina rode straight up to the front door. She dismounted and said to Mr Bennett: 'Will you take the horses to the stables, then join me in the Great Hall.'

'Very good, Miss Zarina,' Mr Bennett replied.

She knew from the expression on his

face and the way he spoke that he was apprehensive of what she was about to do. He was wondering if he would get into a great deal of trouble for allowing her to do it. Zarina, however, was not concerned with Mr Bennett's feelings. She was thinking of herself and the tortures she had suffered all night.

She walked up the steps and into the house and entered the Great Hall where once travellers had received a warm welcome from the Monks who never turned anybody away.

It was filled now with men carrying pictures and pieces of furniture which they were setting down behind an Auctioneer's stand, beside which was a table and a chair. Zarina knew it would be used by his assistant who would take notes of the bids and the names of the buyers.

No one took any notice of her as she walked towards the door which led to the State Rooms. Standing nearby was a servant whom she recognised as having been the Butler at the Priory for many years.

'Good morning, Yates!' she said.

He started when he heard her voice, then smiled. 'I didn't know you were 'ome, Miss Zarina.'

'I only came back from London last night,' Zarina replied. 'Where is His Lordship?'

'I thinks now as he'll be in the Library, Miss,' Yates answered. 'This be a sad day—a very sad day for us all!'

'I must speak to His Lordship,' Zarina said. She hurried off down the passage. Yates in his misery made no effort to escort her. She knew her way. When she reached the Library the door was open and she could see Rolfe staring at the books, which completely covered the windowless walls.

There were two other men there, inspecting the shelves. Zarina guessed that they would be looking for First Editions and ancient Manuscripts which were part of the history of the family.

Rolfe, now the 10th Earl of Linwood, was watching them with an expression which Zarina knew was one of despair.

As she walked up to him he heard her footsteps, turned and gave an exclamation of surprise. 'Zarina! I heard you were in London!'

'I came home yesterday,' Zarina answered, 'and I want to talk to you alone.'

For a moment she thought he was going to refuse. Then he said: 'There is really nothing to say, but come into the Study. I think they have finished in there.'

The Study was next door and Zarina walked ahead of him. When he opened the door she understood what he meant by saying they had finished. The pictures, which had been particularly fine examples of Medieval Art had all been taken down from the walls. The ornaments had gone from the mantelpiece. So had a very fine Regency desk which she remembered the late Earl had always used.

All that remained were the leather chairs and sofas which were each marked with a ticket. They were to be auctioned without actually appearing in the Great Hall.

Rolfe shut the door behind him. Then he

said: 'It is nice to see you, Zarina, but I do not want your pity or your commiserations. There is nothing else I can do about the situation.'

He spoke sharply and Zarina knew by the expression in his eyes how much he was suffering. 'I have come to offer you neither of those things,' she said. 'I have come to make a suggestion which I think will help you and..'

She was about to say 'me' when Rolfe interrupted her. 'Whatever you are going to suggest I do not want to hear it. I do not want charity from you or anybody else!' He spoke furiously.

'If you would let me finish,' Zarina retorted, 'you would understand that I am not offering you charity. What I want is for you to agree to our being engaged to be married.'

Again Rolfe interrupted. 'I do not know what you are saying,' he said, 'but the answer is "No"! I may have sunk very low, but I do not take money from women!'

Zarina walked nearer to him and said:

'If you would stop shouting at me, I want you to understand that I am..begging you to..help me.'

'To help you,' Rolfe asked. 'How can I possibly do that?'

'As I have just said, by allowing us to become engaged to be married.'

'You must be crazy!' Rolfe replied.

'I said "Engaged",' Zarina said, 'because that is all it would be. What I will do in return is to pay Darcy's debts because by becoming my *fiancé* you will protect me from being forced by my Uncle into a marriage to a man I loathe and who will make me utterly and completely miserable.'

Rolfe stared at her before he said: 'Now what is all this about? I may be very dense, but I can make no sense of what you are saying.'

'Then you must be extremely stupid,' Zarina replied. 'It is really quite simple— my Uncle, and you know what he is like, wishes me to marry the Duke of Malnesbury.'

'Which, of course, is a very sensible

idea,' Rolfe said. 'A Duke is always a Duke, and most women would give their eyes to be a Duchess.'

'I am the exception!' Zarina said sharply. Then in a different tone of voice she said quietly: 'Do try to understand, Rolfe. You know how happy Mama and Papa were together and how much they loved each other. Do you really think I want any other sort of marriage except to somebody I love and who loves me?'

'Which of course you will eventually find,' Rolfe said.

'Uncle Alexander said last night that if I did not agree to marry the Duke he would drag me to the altar, or..beat me into..submission.'

'Do you really think he would do that?' Rolfe asked.

'I am sure of it,' Zarina answered. 'He thinks it is not only the best possible thing for me, but also for the family. And, if you remember what Aunt Edith is like, you would know it is her idea of being in Heaven to have me a traditional Lady-of-the-Bedchamber.'

As if he could not help it, Rolfe gave a short laugh. 'It is a miserable story, Zarina,' he said. 'At the same time, I want no part of it.'

'Do you not understand that if Papa was alive he would try to help you. He would also not allow Uncle Alexander to bully me in this degrading manner. I have no one to help me.'

'I am not the right person to do so,' Rolfe said.

'How can you be so unkind? How can you be so cruel, seeing we have known each other since we were children, and the Priory has always been something very precious in my life?'

As if he felt disturbed by the way she was speaking, Rolfe walked across to the window. He stood looking out at the sunshine.

'What is wrong,' Zarina went on, 'in asking you to help me when I am desperate—utterly and completely desperate? I can help you by paying Darcy's debts and sending away all these people who are arriving to get something cheaply which belongs to the Priory and has done for centuries.'

'Have you any idea,' Rolfe asked, 'what Darcy's debts amount to?'

'They are not important,' Zarina answered. 'I have so much money, which of course you know I inherited from my Godmother, that it would be impossible to spend it all, if I lived to be a hundred and fifty!'

'So the stories I have heard about you are true!' Rolfe said. 'They were talking about the fabulous Heiress before I left England, and I found, even on the ship home, people were chattering about your wealth.'

'It is all true,' Zarina said, 'but if I have to share it with a Duke who is old enough to be my grandfather, I shall make a Will leaving it all to a Cats' Home, then drown myself in the stream!'

'Now you are talking over-dramatically,' Rolfe said. 'You know quite well you would do nothing of the sort! In fact you will enjoy wearing the biggest and most glittering tiara at the Opening of Parliament.'

'I have told you—I will not marry him!' Zarina cried. 'Oh, please, Rolfe, help me! I am frightened of Uncle Alexander. I cannot help it! Somehow or other he will get me up the aisle, then there will be nothing I can do but..hope to..die!'

Rolfe's lips tightened and he said: 'Shall I talk to the General? After all, he might have listened to Papa, although I doubt it.'

'I do not think if all the Archangels of Heaven came down and talked to him it would alter his mind. He thinks he knows best what is good for me and is determined that I shall marry the Duke.' Zarina threw out her hands in a gesture of despair.

'Do you really think,' Rolfe asked, 'he would pay any attention if you told him you were engaged to a Peer without a penny in his pocket?' He looked at her seriously before he added: 'Or a roof over his head—after today.'

'You will have the Priory and all it contains,' Zarina said softly, 'and it will

give me time to try to find a way out.'
Rolfe did not speak and she said after a moment: 'I was awake all night trying to think how I could run away and where I could go, but I am sure it would be a mistake to go..alone.'

'Of course it would!' Rolfe answered. 'How could you possibly look after yourself and, besides, if anyone found out who you were, you would have every Fortune-Hunter grasping at you for what they could get.'

'I am aware of that,' Zarina agreed, 'and therefore I have to go away with someone like yourself until Uncle Alexander capitulates and admits that he cannot choose my husband for me.'

'I am leaving tomorrow for India,' Rolfe said. 'I have no intention of staying here once the place is empty and sold.'

'I will come with you!'

Rolfe walked back from the window. 'Try to be sensible, Zarina,' he said. 'How can you possibly come with me without a Chaperone? You know as well as I do that your reputation would be in ribbons.'

'Then instead of pretending that you are my fiancé,' Zarina said, 'I will pretend to be your wife. No one would question our position while we are travelling, and unless Uncle Alexander is clairvoyant, he will not know where we have gone.' She paused as if she was working it out in her mind. 'I will tell him I have gone to France with you to stay with some of your relatives who want to meet your fiancée.'

Rolfe put his hands up to his forehead. 'Do listen, Zarina,' he said. 'I cannot agree to this—of course I cannot. It is no use you trying to talk me into it.'

'Then how else can you help me?' she asked. 'Surely, as we have known each other so long, you can accept my word that I have no wish to marry you, as you have no wish to marry me.' She paused a moment, to look at him pleadingly. 'What I am suggesting is a strict business deal. I will pay your debts if you will spirit me away for a few months, by which time Uncle Alexander will give up the chase.'

'You cannot be sure of that,' Rolfe said.

'Well, at least we will have tried to make him realise that I will not marry the Duke,' Zarina said. 'And if the Duke thinks I am engaged to you, he will not want to marry me.'

'I suppose that depends on how keen he is,' Rolfe answered.

'I am not concerned with him in any way,' Zarina said passionately, 'but with myself. Help me, oh, please help me! If I was drowning you would have to try to save me. This is definitely worse.'

Rolfe walked across the Study and back again. 'I honestly never imagined in my wildest dreams that you would turn up and make such a suggestion.'

'You must be sensible enough to realise that it is a gift from the Gods,' Zarina said. 'I have brought Bennett with me and he has my cheque-book.'

Quite suddenly Rolfe laughed, and this time it was a genuine expression of humour. 'Zarina, you are incorrigible!' he exclaimed. 'How can you have hatched up such a ridiculous plot? However I appreciate that you are in somewhat of a fix, if, as you say, the General has set his heart on you becoming a Duchess.'

'Of course he has,' Zarina said, 'and although he says the Duke is in love with me, I very much doubt if he would condescend to mix his blue-blood with mine, if it was not for my American dollars.'

'Young women of your age should not be cynical,' Rolfe replied. 'They should view the world through rose-coloured spectacles.'

'I do not want to view the Duke through anything!' Zarina said crossly. Rolfe did not speak and after a moment she asked: 'What time are you leaving tomorrow and from where are we sailing?'

'I have not yet said I will take you with me,' Rolfe answered.

'But you will,' Zarina stated. 'You cannot just abandon me to my fate, and as Jenkins said this morning, your father would turn in his grave if he knew you were selling the Priory.'

'What else can I do?' Rolfe asked apologetically. 'I cannot imagine how it was possible that Darcy should have so many debts owed to so many people and actually have nothing whatever to show for them.'

'What did he buy?' Zarina asked.

'It is not a question of purchasing anything,' Rolfe replied. 'He spent a fortune on women, about which you should know nothing. He gave them jewellery, horses, carriages, furs, everything you can name.' He paused and then went on: 'His parties, which ended up rowdy, with an enormous number of breakages, took place night after night, week after week.'

'I suppose he enjoyed himself,' Zarina said.

'I can only hope so,' Rolfe replied, 'but I have been left to sort out the mess he has created. I can assure you that is not amusing!'

'I can understand what you feel,' Zarina replied. 'At the same time, Luck, or perhaps your Guardian Angel, has thought of a solution, and that is..me!'

Rolfe drew in his breath, then he said:

'Let me make one effort to speak to your Uncle.'

'You must be very conceited if you think Uncle Alexander would pay any attention to you. He has always been a Martinet. He has always believed that everybody else is wrong, and he is right.' She gave a little sigh before she went on: 'Ever since I have lived with him I have felt sorry for the soldiers under his command, and sorry for myself.' She clasped her hands together as she said: 'I have to..escape, so let us stop arguing about it. You will pick me up tomorrow morning. What time are you leaving?'

'Very early,' Rolfe answered.

'I will be ready and I can only hope that Uncle Alexander will be so incensed at my having paid Darcy's debts that he will not suspect for a moment that you and I are actually running away.'

'I thought we were supposed to be engaged?' Rolfe remarked.

'I shall leave a letter telling him how happy we are,' Zarina said.

'Do you really think you are going to

get away with this?' Rolfe asked.

'When I asked you to pretend to be engaged to me,' Zarina replied, 'I did not know that you would be leaving for India tomorrow morning. That now seems to be a perfect getaway. I will be out of reach of Uncle Alexander, especially if he is looking for me in France.' She smiled before she added: 'It would be some time before he learns that we have gone to India.'

'Seventeen days, or rather nineteen, as I am going to Calcutta,' Rolfe said.

'I suppose it will be hot,' Zarina remarked reflectively. 'I shall need my summer clothes.'

There was a pause. Then Rolfe said in a hard voice: 'If you come with me—and let me make this very clear from the beginning—I do not intend to spend your money on myself.' He was glowering at her. 'I am travelling in a Cargo-Ship which will be uncomfortable and dirty. If you come with me as my wife you will behave as my wife, and you will spend *my* money—not yours!' There was silence before he added: 'You can stay

68

until you can find somewhere better to go and which will undoubtedly be much more comfortable.'

'I am coming with you,' Zarina said. 'If you want to be unpleasant about my money, I cannot stop you. But I think it is extremely stupid and rather bad taste.'

'I have some pride left!' Rolfe argued. 'If I have to be kept by a woman, I would rather throw myself overboard!'

'Who is being over-dramatic now?' Zarina asked.

Rolfe looked embarrassed. 'You are right,' he answered, 'but you do realise that not only your Uncle will think I am the biggest Fortune-Hunter there has ever been, but so will all my friends—and my enemies.'

'They will change their tune,' Zarina said lightly, 'when we break off our engagement and put in *The Times* that our marriage will not now take place.' She rose from the sofa on which she had been sitting. 'Now I think you had better come to talk to Bennett and decide how you are going to send all these people away, and of course settle their bills.'

She glanced up at Rolfe as she spoke and for a moment they just looked at one another. Then he said quietly: 'One thing I swear to you, Zarina: somehow, in some way, God knows how, I will pay you back—every penny of the money you are spending on me and the Priory today.' He made a little gesture with his hand. 'It may take me a thousand years—but I will do it!'

'Very well,' Zarina answered, 'and I shall be eternally grateful to you for having saved me from the Duke. You can think of yourself as a White Knight killing the Dragon, and of course, White Knights always gave themselves impossible tasks.'

'I am serious,' Rolfe said.

She smiled at him and he realised there was a dimple on either side of her mouth.

'Of course you are,' she answered, 'and as serious people are always terribly boring, I hope you will be a little more amusing as we pass down the Red Sea.'

She walked towards the door as she

spoke. As Rolfe followed her he said: 'All I can say, Zarina, is that the General showed some common sense when he said you should be beaten into submission. It is obviously something you managed to avoid as a child!'

Chapter Three

When they left the Study, although the Sale was not scheduled to start until two o'clock, they found the Great Hall was filling up. Men were examining the pictures. They pulled one after another from against the wall where they had been arranged. They were also arguing with each other as to the date of a piece of furniture, or saying it was wrongly marked in the catalogue.

Zarina saw Mr Bennett at the end of the Hall and walked towards him. As she did so she said to Rolfe: 'You must come to meet Mr Bennett. He will pay all the bills and will cope with everything.'

They reached Mr Bennett and Rolfe held out his hand. 'How are you, Bennett?' he enquired. 'it is a long time since we last met.'

'It's good to see Your Lordship,' Mr Bennett replied. 'I hope you had an enjoyable time abroad.'

'Very interesting' Rolfe replied.

'I think we had better go into the Abbot's Room,' Zarina suggested.

Rolfe did not argue and she led the way to the Abbot's Room, which was behind the Great Hall. It was large and comfortable, panelled with beautifully carved oak. The windows looked out onto a Court Yard. This was in the centre of the Priory instead of at the front of the building. A quick glance showed Zarina that the Court-Yard was full of weeds. The statue in the middle, which was of the original Priory, wanted cleaning.

Rolfe shut the door and she said to Mr Bennett: 'I suggest you sit down while I tell you what is to be done.'

He looked at her a little apprehensively,

but did as she suggested.

She also sat down in one of the chairs which had not been taken into the Great Hall. 'I have told His Lordship,' Zarina began quietly, 'that we will pay all the bills incurred by Mr Darcy. It will be announced that the Auction Sale will not now take place and the people who are now trying to find a bargain will have to go home without one.' She paused for a moment before she went on: 'Also the Priory itself is not for sale. I want you to see that everything is put back in its place and that the wages owing to the servants and those on the Estate are paid.'

She glanced at Rolfe as she spoke. His mouth was set in a tight line, his chin was square and she knew he was incensed at what he was hearing. At the same time, he knew that he was helpless and could do nothing about it.

'What I am going to tell you,' Zarina went on, 'is completely confidential, and you must promise me on your honour that you will not repeat it to anyone, especially my Uncle.'

'I must tell you, Miss Zarina,' Mr Bennett said, 'that the General will very much disapprove of what you are doing.'

'I am well aware of that,' Zarina replied, 'but the General has made plans for me which I have already told him I refuse to accept.' She hesitated for a moment as to whether she should tell Mr Bennett the whole truth, then thought it would be a mistake. 'What I am confiding in you,' she continued after a moment, 'is that His Lordship and I are engaged to be married.'

Mr Bennett looked startled, but he managed to say very warmly: 'Then, of course, I wish you every happiness, Miss Zarina, and congratulations, Your Lordship. I know, Miss Zarina, it is something which would have pleased your father and mother.'

'That is what I think,' Zarina answered, 'but I know it will displease the General, and that is why His Lordship and I are going away.'

'Going away?' Mr Bennett asked. 'How soon?'

'Tomorrow,' Zarina replied, 'and I am afraid you will have to bear the brunt of my Uncle's anger, but you must convince him that you know nothing and therefore cannot tell him where we have gone.'

'Are you intending, Miss Zarina, to inform the General that you are going away?'

'I am writing a letter which he will read after I have left,' Zarina replied. 'Otherwise there might be a scene in which he might prevent me forcibly from leaving the country.'

Mr Bennett put his hand up to his forehead. 'You are making things very difficult for me, Miss Zarina,' he complained.

'That is not entirely true, Mr Bennett,' Zarina said. 'If we get down to bare facts, I employ you, I pay your wages, you run my House and my Estate and follow my instructions.'

'Of course that is true,' Mr Bennett agreed.

'Therefore, my Uncle has no jurisdiction over you, and has no right to accuse you

of anything, but obeying my instructions.'
There was a short pause and she glanced
again at Rolfe before she said: 'What I
am going to ask you to do as soon as
we have gone is to run this Estate for
His Lordship in the same way as you do
mine.' She could see that Mr Bennett was
taken aback, but she went on: 'We have
complete confidence in you and in any
changes you may make. Of course you
will keep the Priory in the same state of
repair as you keep my house.'

She smiled before she added: 'I want it
to look exactly as it did when I was a
child and thought it was the most beautiful
building anyone could see.'

She had a feeling as she spoke that Rolfe
was longing to interrupt and say that he
would not accept her money where it
concerned his home. Quickly, before he
could speak, she said, still looking at Mr
Bennett: 'His Lordship and I are well
aware that all the old servants who have
been here for many years are extremely
worried that they will be turned away
without a pension and have nowhere to

go.' She paused a moment to smile at him, before she added: 'His Lordship will of course reassure them as much as he can before he leaves. But it is up to you to see that they are well provided for and have enough help to keep the Priory as perfect as we want it to be.'

'I will do my best, Miss Zarina,' Mr Bennett said, 'but you understand, there may be difficulties.'

'Only where my Uncle is concerned,' Zarina said, 'and, as I am now His Lordship's fiancée, he now has no power over me.' Mr Bennett looked a little doubtful and she went on: 'Anyway, I have no intention of telling him our address and therefore he cannot interfere with our engagement.'

'I think, Miss Zarina, if you will excuse me for saying so, you should give me your address in case anything occurred which would be impossible for me to manage without your agreement.'

Zarina looked at Rolfe. 'I think that is a sensible idea,' he said, speaking for the first time. 'I am, however not certain where we will be in India.'

'In India!' Mr Bennett exclaimed. 'If you're going back there, My Lord, I feel I must definitely be able to get in touch with you in an emergency.'

'Very well,' Rolfe said, 'but I have no idea exactly where Miss Zarina and I will be. Therefore you must write to us at the Viceroy's House in Calcutta. I will arrange for any letters to be forwarded.'

'Thank you,' Mr Bennett said, 'thank you very much, My Lord, but I'll do my best not to trouble you.'

'Now that is settled,' Zarina said brightly, 'I suggest we all have something to eat. I have had no breakfast, and I am very hungry.'

'I will go and see to it,' Mr Bennett said, 'and perhaps it would be best if you eat whatever is available in here.'

'Yes, of course,' Zarina agreed.

Mr Bennett went from the room and Rolfe said: 'You have certainly taken over in a big way!'

'I knew it would upset you,' Zarina

replied, 'but it would be a mistake to let the place go to rack and ruin. You can already see the weeds in the Court-Yard, and the statue that always looked so impressive has not been cleaned.'

'I believe some of the younger men left before I returned,' Rolfe said. 'There was no money to pay them when my father died. Although I started to come home as soon as I heard of my brother's death, I was in the North of India and it therefore took some time to get South.'

'Is that where we are going now?' Zarina asked.

'It is where I want to go,' Rolfe replied, 'because I had just heard that in Nepal there are some exceedingly interesting manuscripts in a Monastery that is out of reach of the usual men who are interested in that sort of thing.'

'Ancient manuscripts!' Zarina exclaimed. 'I had no idea that you knew anything about them.'

'In other words,' Rolfe said, 'you thought I was an ignoramus, or just a pleasure-seeker like Darcy.'

'I did not think either of those things about you,' Zarina said. 'I had an idea you were just travelling for adventure.'

'That is exactly what I am travelling for,' Rolfe said. 'There are so many things I want to see, and so many things I want to find. I was, in fact, going to bring the manuscripts back to the Library here.'

'Thank goodness that need not be sold!' Zarina said. 'I remember your father showing me some of the early editions which were exquisitely illustrated and of course, you would have got a large sum of money for one of the first volumes of Chaucer.'

'Now they are yours!' Rolfe said in a hard voice.

'On the contrary, they are what I have paid you for saving me from the Duke.'

'I think, if we tell the truth, you have been cheated!'

'The only thing it is impossible to estimate in hard cash is me!' Zarina retorted. 'And as I rate myself very highly, I think I got a cheap deal.'

Rolfe laughed as if he could not

help himself. Then, before he could say anything, the old Butler, Yates, came in carrying a table-cloth. 'I 'ears, M'Lord,' he said, ''as you'd like something t'eat. Mrs Blossom's doing 'er best, but she says there be very little in th' larder.'

'We will be grateful for anything,' Rolfe said, 'but Miss Bryden says she is hungry.'

'We'll do what we can, M'Lord,' Yates said. He pulled out from a wall an ancient table that was in need of repair, which was the reason, Zarina could see, why it had not been taken with the other furniture into the Great Hall.

When Yates left the room she said to Rolfe: 'When do you intend to tell them that the Sale will not now take place.'

'When they are all here,' he replied. 'There is no point in saying the same thing twice.'

'I expect they will be disappointed.'

'I hope so,' he answered. 'I hate the type of Buyer on these occasions who is determined to get a bargain at all costs.'

Again he was speaking bitterly. Zarina could understand that what was occurring was hurting his pride. She looked back to when she was a child. She had always thought in a childish way that the two boys from the Priory gave themselves 'airs'. When she considered that they had one of the finest houses, the best horses and, she had to admit, the finest Estate in the County, it was not surprising. They had both been to Eton and both had gone on to Oxford. They had been pursued not only by all the prettiest girls, but also by all the ambitious mothers. Darcy had gone to London and quickly earned a reputation as a *Roué*. Rolfe, on the other hand, was continually abroad. Now, when she thought back, she remembered the Earl complaining to her parents that he saw very little of his two sons. Of course he had been lonely. Therefore the friendship that her father and mother had offered him was very precious.

Following her own train of thought she said unexpectedly to Rolfe: 'Do you really care so much for your home? You spent a great deal of time away from it, after you left Oxford.'

'The Priory has always meant to me more than I can put into words,' Rolfe replied. 'But I realised from the time I left the cradle that it would eventually be Darcy's and that I would have to make my home somewhere else, and with very little money.'

There was no need for him to explain to Zarina that in all aristocratic families the eldest son received everything. His younger brothers could only be given what could be spared, which was sometimes very little. It ensured, however, that the great Estates could be kept up.

The Head of a family was not only of tremendous importance, he was also in control. Now Zarina understood why Rolfe had tried to find interests away from England, where he was very much subservient to his elder brother.

As if he could read her thoughts, Rolfe said: 'I never imagined—never dreamt for a moment that this would be mine. When I knew it was, it was an agony to know I could not keep it.'

'I can understand that,' Zarina said

quickly, 'and now we have to make the Priory perfect for you.'

'I shall try to do that, once my debt to you is paid,' Rolfe said.

'I consider it paid already, or rather, we will believe that once I am away from my Uncle. If you want to make heavy weather of it, you must do so.'

Zarina spoke sharply and Rolfe said quickly: 'I am grateful. I am sorry if I do not sound so, but I *am* grateful. Yet it goes against every instinct in my body to accept charity from anyone, let alone a woman.'

As if he did not wish to discuss it any more, he walked out of the room leaving the door open. Zarina knew he had gone to see what was happening in the Great Hall, but for the moment she was not particularly interested. She was busy planning in her mind how she could get away tomorrow without making her Uncle suspicious of what she was going to do.

Rolfe came back when Yates brought in the food. There was cold ham, but not very much of it and there were two bowls containing hot rabbit soup, and a piece of Stilton cheese.

Yates was apologetic that there was not more to offer them at such short notice. Neither Zarina nor Rolfe, however, were particularly interested in what they ate as long as they were no longer hungry.

Zarina had just sat down at the table when Rolfe gave an exclamation and went from the room. He came back a few minutes later with a bottle of claret in his hand. 'I just remembered this,' he said. 'There is nothing else in the cellar which has not been marked to be sold, but I did reserve this very good claret of my father's (for myself). I was keeping if for my dinner tonight.'

'I never touch alcohol as a rule,' Zarina said, 'but I think we should both drink a toast to our future and that we shall be lucky in what happens after we leave here.'

'I will certainly drink to that!' Rolfe said. he poured out the claret and they toasted each other solemnly across the table.

Then Zarina started on the soup and ate

some of the home-cured ham.

When Yates had left the room to fetch them some coffee to finish the meal, Zarina said: 'What time are you collecting me tomorrow morning?'

'As early as possible,' Rolfe replied. 'I intended to take the 'Milk Train' to London. It passes the Halt at five thirty and I will be at Tilbury before noon.'

'If I am ready at four forty-five,' Zarina said, 'it will certainly be before the General comes on parade.'

'Where shall I pick you up?' Rolfe asked. 'It would not be wise to come to the front door.'

'Of course not,' Zarina replied. 'Stop at the end of the stables beside the paddocks. I doubt if even the stable-boys will be up as early as that, but if they do see us it will not matter.'

'No, of course not,' Rolfe agreed, 'and when they know we have run away they will doubtless think it very romantic—something they would like to do themselves.'

'We must not make any mistakes,' Zarina

said in a serious voice. She was thinking how furious her Uncle would be when he learnt that she had escaped. She was quite certain that, if he knew where she had gone, he would try to reach her somehow. Then she thought it was very unlikely that the General would think of going to Tilbury if she said in her letter that she was going to France. He would probably post off to Dover, by which time they would be on the high seas and on their way to India.

They drank their coffee and Rolfe had a second glass of claret before he took his watch from his waist-coat pocket. 'It is a few minutes to two,' he said, 'and the Hall ought to be full by now.' He rose from the table.

'Good luck!' Zarina said.

He smiled at her and walked away.

She stopped behind to thank Yates and say she would go to see Mrs Blossom. Then she moved along the passage which led to the back of the Great Hall. There was another door which was open. She stood looking at the crowd which was moving in front of the Auctioneer's stand.

She could see Rolfe talking to a man on it who was obviously the Auctioneer. She could also see Mr Bennett standing just behind him. The Auctioneer's Assistant was already seated at the table. On Rolfe's insistence, the Auctioneer, looking astonished, stepped down and Rolfe took his place. He stood up, looking very tall, and in his own way, Zarina thought, as handsome as his brother. Suddenly there was silence. She thought there must be more than a hundred people in the Great Hall and they were all looking up at Rolfe. She could see in the front of the crowd there were men who she was quite certain had come from London. They would grab the proceeds from the sale as soon as it was over. There was something very unpleasant about them with their sharp eyes and hard mouths. They would not have hesitated, Zarina thought, if it was to their advantage, or just for revenge, to have sent Darcy to prison.

'Gentlemen,' Rolfe began in a voice that seemed to ring out round the walls of the Great Hall. 'I am the Earl of Linwood, and

I would have like to have welcomed you here today on a more auspicious occasion.' He paused and looked round the crowd before continuing: 'You have come, some of you from a long distance, to purchase the contents of the Priory and the Priory itself. I must therefore apologise to you, that your journey was unnecessary and, if it had been possible, I would have saved you from making it.'

There was a murmur of astonishment throughout the Hall before Rolfe went on: 'I can however inform you that the money you are owed by my brother will now be paid in full. If you will present your bills to Mr Bennett, who is now seated at the table in front of me, he will make you out cheques which I promise you will be cashed immediately when you take them to Coutts Bank in the Haymarket.'

Now there was a rising sound of astonishment until one of the men in front of the others, shouted out: 'Why weren't we told of this before an' 'ow do we know that you're not just trickin' us?'

'There are plenty of people here to

vouch for the fact that I am the Earl of Linwood,' Rolfe replied, 'and I can only give you my word that the cheques you receive for what you are owed will be met without any difficulty.'

'I'd like t'be certain o' that!' the man who had spoken before shouted. ''Ow can we be sure this ain't a trick to make us go 'ome, so's you can sell what's 'ere to someone else, an' we'll get nothin'?'

'That might 'appen,' the man next to him said.

The others began to join in, their voices rising. They appeared to Zarina to have a threatening look about them. It was obvious that Rolfe was not certain what he could say but he had to convince the creditors that the money which had not been there yesterday was here today. They must have gone very deeply into his brother's finances and doubtless also those of his father before they got to the stage of threatening Darcy with imprisonment.

Mr Bennett, who had taken the place of the Auctioneer's Assistant, was looking worried. He had a cheque-book in his hand that did not assure those who were owed large sums of money that a cheque would be met when they presented it.

'We wanna go on wi' the auction as promised!' the men who had been aggressive from the beginning shouted. 'We're not leavin' here wi' out somethin' in our hands!'

'Yeah, that's right!' another man shouted.

There was a murmur of asset from the other creditors.

It was then Zarina knew what she must do. She pushed her way through the crowd until she reached the Auctioneer's stand. It was raised about three feet from the ground and looked almost like a pulpit with two steps leading up to it. She climbed them to stand beside Rolfe. When he realised she was there he said in a low voice: 'Do not get embroiled in this.'

'They are not going to believe you unless I tell them who I am,' she said. 'Introduce me.'

He momentarily hesitated. Then the men who were making trouble thought Rolfe was prevaricating and shouted again for the Auctioneer. Forced to take the only action possible, Rolfe reluctantly waved his hand for silence. 'Because you are doubting my word,' he said, 'I want to introduce you to Miss Zarina Bryden, who has honoured me by consenting to become my wife.'

For a moment there was silence, then a gasp of astonishment. At the same time, Zarina heard quite audibly several people say: 'The Heiress! That's the Heiress!' It was the word she had heard so often repeated by one after another of the people standing in front of them.

For a moment they just whispered amongst themselves. Then the man who had made all the trouble in the first place, said: 'If Miss Bryden's backin' you, then that's good enough for us.'

'Of course I am backing him,' Zarina said, 'and I hope you will all wish us Good Luck and happiness in the future.' There was no need to say more. The men who had started the trouble surged towards Mr Bennett, holding out their bills so that he could see how much they were owed.

Zarina got down from the Auctioneer's stand and Rolfe followed her. Then, as they started to move, a number of women in the Hall came hurrying up to shake their hands and wish them luck. They were followed by men who worked on the Estate. There were also several old pensioners who must have found it a long way to walk from the village.

They were Rolfe's people and they had a lot to say to him. After a few minutes, Zarina moved away from his side. She thought it would be a mistake to impose herself too much upon him. He was already resenting that he was forced to accept her money. She thought instead that this was a good moment to look at the Priory.

Although the rooms had been stripped of so much that she remembered, it would still be comforting to think that everything would be back in place and the Priory would look as it always had.

It was too difficult at the moment for Zarina to leave the Great Hall by the door which led to the Library where she had been this morning. Instead, she went in the other direction. She passed the Abbot's Room and went on towards the Chapel. She went in and saw it was just as beautiful as she remembered it had always been.

Those who had arranged the Auction had not touched the gold Cross on top of the altar. Nor had they moved the candlesticks which were very ancient and valuable.

Zarina knew the reason why they had been left. A great number of people were too superstitious to touch or remove anything from a Chapel that was consecrated. She thought the Auctioneer very likely intended to leave the Chapel furnishings to those who bought the Priory. They could risk the bad luck of removing them, if indeed that was their intention.

The beautifully carved *Prie-Dieu* was still in front of the altar steps and she knelt on it. She thanked God for showing her the way by which she could escape from the Duke. She begged Him to protect both her and Rolfe on their voyage to India. She was not sure what would happen then. She wondered if she would be able to leave him without being afraid that the Duke would pounce on her.

'Help me..help me..God,' she prayed. 'For without You and..without Rolfe to ..protect me I will be..very frightened.'

When she opened her eyes a shaft of sunlight shone through the stained-glass window above the altar. It touched the golden Cross and she thought also that it touched her head. It seemed like a sign that God had heard her.

Somehow, whatever happened in the future, she could be safe.

Chapter Four

Zarina stayed in the Chapel for some time. When she left she thought she would go to see Mrs Blossom as she had promised. It would obviously take a long time for the people in the Hall to show their bills and to have cheques made out to them.

She had not gone very far when she saw two men coming towards her. She recognised one as the man who had made the disturbance in the Hall. He had, it would seem, as he was very pushy, got paid first. He was a coarse-looking man, but flashily dressed. He had what she thought was a deceitful face which no one would trust.

She was just about to pass them when they blocked her way. 'We've bin lookin' for you, Miss Bryden,' the flashy man said.

Zarina raised her eye-brows. 'For me?' she questioned.

'Yes, we've got somethin' to show yer.'

Zarina wondered what it could be and wanted to refuse. Then, as they walked beside her, she felt it would be rude to do so.

They moved along the passage until they had nearly reached the Kitchen. Then the flashy man opened the door of a room she had never been in before. She suspected it was used, when the late Earl was alive, by his Secretary. There was a desk in the centre of the room, and maps on the walls. A number of black tin boxes which could have contained references to the Farms and Estate were piled in one corner. There was nobody in the room.

Zarina was just about to ask why they had brought her there when she realised that the flashy man had closed the door behind him in a somewhat aggressive manner. 'What is it?' she asked sharply. 'What do you want me to see?'

'Now, it jest so 'appens, Miss Bryden,' the flashy man replied, 'that when I were paid wot I was owed in t'Hall I finds I keeps me money in Coutts Bank, same as yer do.'

Zarina stiffened. She did not like the over-familiar manner in which he was speaking to her.

'Now, wot I'm thinkin',' the flashy man went on, 'is that a rich young lady like yerself, 'as so much money that yer wouldn't miss a little more.'

'I do not understand what you are saying,' Zarina said, 'and I wish to leave.'

She turned, only to find that the other man who had not spoken was standing in front of the door. He told her without words, that he would not allow her to pass.

She hesitated and the flashy man said: 'It's quite simple, Miss Bryden. All yer 'ave t'do is t'sign this 'ere cheque, which is mine, an' I'm quite sure th' Bank'll honour it. After all, why should they refuse when they've got piles of yer money at their disposal?'

He was jeering at her and Zarina said angrily: 'I have no wish to continue this conversation and I wish to find His Lordship.'

'This'll only take yer a few seconds,' the flashy man said, 'all yer've got t'do is t'put yer signature t'this.'

He put a cheque down on the table as he spoke. Almost without meaning to Zarina read what was written on it. It was made out for the sum of £20,000.

'If you think I am going to sign that, you are very much mistaken!' she said. 'In any case, I am quite sure the Bank would be suspicious if you presented a cheque for such a large amount.'

'I thinks that be very unlikely considerin' 'ow much 'Is Nibs' debts come to,' the flashy man replied. 'If yer pain' for 'Is Lordship, as I suspect, then it's costin' yer a pretty penny an' another twenty-thou' 'ere or there be of no consequence.'

'It is of consequence to me,' Zarina replied, 'and what you are trying to do is not only fraudulent, but criminal!'

'Well, if that's yer last word,' the flashy man said slowly, 'I'm afraid I'll 'ave t'be a wee bit more persuasive.'

As he spoke he put a handkerchief swiftly over Zarina's head and gagged her. She started to struggle. The other man came from where he had been standing in front of the door to pinion her arms. She found she was helpless. Then the flashy man brought from his pocket a long silver chain. Zarina recognised it as the sort of chain which coachmen used, not only to keep a trunk in place, but also to padlock it so that it cannot be stolen. The flashy man whipped it round her waist and her arms then tied the ends. She could not fight herself free of it.

'Open the door, Bill,' the flashy man said, 'an' make sure the coast is clear.'

Bill did as he was told, looking up and down the corridor. Then the flashy man pulled Zarina forward and both men propelled her along. She thought of throwing herself down on the floor, but she knew they would then drag her along. It might be just as easy for them to carry her. She knew, however, that in this part of the Priory, where the Kitchen was situated, Mrs Blossom would be working at the stove. The rest of the servants, and they were only the older ones, would be at the front of the house where all the people were.

The man, with Zarina between them, had not gone far before they turned a corner. She realised with a sense of shock that they were heading for the cellars. She had only been in them once or twice when the boys had taken her there as a child. She knew, however, the cellars were vast and went deep down under the building itself.

The door was open and she saw that the wine, ready to be sold, had been ticketed like the furniture. There was not a great deal of it. When they passed through the first cellar into the second it was almost empty and it was in darkness until Bill produced a lantern which was lit and hidden in a corner.

The lantern told Zarina that the two men had been here before. They must have decided this was where they would take her if she did not agree to sign the cheque.

The other man now led the way through the second cellar which was long. Then there was another which had a low ceiling and was completely empty.

She began to feel very afraid. If they were going to leave her in this cellar she thought it very unlikely that anyone would find her. Why should they when there was nothing in these last cellars and only the first one was in use?

The third cellar ended in what she thought at first was just a brick wall. Yet there was a door which was small and narrow and creaked when Bill opened it.

The fourth cellar was much smaller than the others and, Zarina thought, somewhat damp. There was not a bottle or a barrel in it, but in the wall there was what appeared to be an open vault made of a dark stone. The doors were heavy and as they reached them Zarina realised why they had brought her there.

They propped her against the door and, undoing the link-chain round her waist, slipped it through an aperture in the door itself. The flashy man fastened the padlock and locked it. He put the key into his pocket and said: 'Bill an' me are just off to get a bite t'eat. We'll be back in two or three hours' time. Then I thinks as 'ow yer'll have changed yer mind 'bout that cheque. If yer don't, yer may be very sorry.'

Zarina did not speak.

He stood looking at her in the light of the lantern before he added: 'Ye're a pretty piece an' now I comes t'think o'it, it might be easier to make yer more accomodatin' in a different way!' The way he spoke and the leer in his eyes made Zarina shudder.

'Come on, Alf,' Bill said. 'Leave 'er t'think it over.'

'All right,' Alf replied, somewhat reluctantly. ''Bye, 'bye, pretty lady, an' don't forget me 'til I comes back.' He laughed unpleasantly. He and Bill went out of the vault, closing the door behind them.

Zarina heard them go up the steps, moving away until there was nothing but silence. She thought how stupid she had been to go with the men when they had first suggested it. It was, however, too late now for regrets. She also thought with horror of what would happen when they returned. Even if she signed the cheque she had the feeling they might leave her here to decay.

'What does twenty thousand pounds matter?' she asked herself, 'when it is a question of life or death?'

'I shall die..I shall die here!' she thought frantically, 'and no one will..ever know what..happened to..me.'

She twisted and turned, but the chain round her waist and arms was too strong.

She knew however hard she pulled, she could not break it. She tried to get her arms free, but that too was impossible and she only hurt herself by trying.

It was then she realised that she could rub the back of her head against the door of the vault to which she was tied to try and dislodge the gag. She rubbed it backwards and forwards. Finally, when she felt the whole thing was pointless, she managed to get her mouth free, then her chin. It was at least a little better than being gagged.

At the same time, she was sensible enough to know that however much she might scream or shout, no one would hear her. She remembered now her father saying that the Priory was very strongly built. It had stood for three hundred years, so it could easily stand for another three hundred.

'What..shall I..do? What can..I do?' Zarina asked herself. She thought of the sunshine that had come through the stained-glass window of the Chapel. It had seemed like an omen. Only prayer would help her now. 'Help me..help me..God,' she prayed. She also sent a plea to her father. She knew he would be furious at the predicament in which she now found herself.

She tried to think how soon it would be before Rolfe realised she was missing. He would be busy in the Great Hall for a long time, if he was helping Mr Bennett with the debts. He would then tell the Auctioneer's men and those he employed to put the pictures and furniture back from where they had taken them. They had not moved any of the wine so there was no reason to hope that anyone would look for her in the cellars.

'Rolfe will think I have gone home,' she told herself. Then she remembered that Mr Bennett had come with her and would expect her to return with him. At least, when he went to fetch his own horse he would see *Kingfisher* in the stable.

'Please, God..please..' she prayed. At the same time, she was feeling the cold and growing more and more afraid.

It must have been an hour later, or

longer, for Zarina had lost all sense of time, when she heard a slight noise. It was only very slight and far away. She listened, afraid for a moment it was nothing human. Perhaps it was a rat. She was certain they existed somewhere deep down underground.

Then the sound came again and it struck her that perhaps somebody was opening the doors of the other vaults.

'Someone!' The word seemed to jump into her mind and tell her it would be Alf and his friend Bill. They would demand that she sign the cheque. If she did, would they set her free? She was intelligent enough to doubt it. They would leave her here a prisoner while they went off to London.

Once they had the money in their hands they were not likely to worry themselves as to what happened to her. There was, too, every likelihood that they would kill her before they left. Then she could not give evidence against them.

The handkerchief with which Alf had gagged her was still round her neck.

Would he pull it a little tighter? She felt a scream coming to her lips. It was then she was aware that there were footsteps just outside the vault. In another minutes she would see Alf and Bill, yet surprisingly the footsteps had stopped and it occurred to her that she had heard not two men walking, but one.

Suddenly a shaft of lightning swept through her. Perhaps it was not them, but somebody looking for her! Rolfe! Could it be Rolfe! For a moment it was impossible for her to speak. Then her voice strangely unlike her own cried:

'Help..help! Please..help..me!'

The sound seemed to ring round the vault and echo as it did so.

Then a voice called: 'Zarina! Are you there? Where are you?'

It was Rolfe!

For a moment she felt she could not reply because of the wonder of it. 'I..am here..I am..here!' She heard him move forward to the small door. He pulled it open and bent his head to walk in. He was carrying a lantern in his hand and he lifted it above his head.

Zarina felt as if he was clothed in shining armour and there was a halo round his head. 'Oh..Rolfe..R..Rolfe..!' she said in a broken voice. The tears started to run down her cheeks.

Rolfe put the lantern down on the floor and in two steps reached her side. 'What the devil has been going on?' he asked.

Zarina could only murmur incoherently: 'You..are here..you are..h..here! I thought.. I would..die! They..left me..here..but they are..coming back.'

'They? Who are "they"?' Rolfe asked.

'Two men..who wanted me..to sign..a cheque for..twenty thousand..pounds!' Zarina managed to reply.

Rolfe was trying to undo the chain round her waist, but the padlock was a large one. 'I cannot do this by myself,' he said, 'I shall have to fetch help.'

'No..no..please..' Zarina cried. 'I..cannot ..bear the thought..of anybody else..knowing what has..happened.' She thought how humiliating it would be. It would be awful if the servants or anyone else realised she had been tied up and blackmailed. It was the sort of story that would go all over the County and people would laugh. At the same time, they would think it served her right for having so much money.

As if Rolfe understood what she was feeling he said: 'Wait a minute! I saw something as I came in.' He picked up the lantern and as he went through the door he said: 'I will only be a minute or so.'

She heard him hurrying back the way he had come. He must have gone as far as the second cellar before she heard him returning. She was holding her breath as she listened because she was so afraid of losing him. The tears were still wet on her cheeks.

Rolfe came back with a large axe in his hand. It was used for opening the barrels. He put down the lantern before he said: 'You must bend forward as much as you can, otherwise what I am going to do will shake you.'

'All that..matters is..that I should..be free,' Zarina answered. She did as he told her. She saw him raise the axe high above his head, then brought it down hard on the chain. At the same time, it broke part of the door of the vault which fell to the ground with a crash.

Zarina was free! She managed to shake off the chain, rubbing her arms where they had been hurt by the tightness of it. Even as she did so, she suddenly felt as if she was going to faint. She must have swayed because Rolfe put his arm round her. 'It is all right,' he said, 'it is over and I will kill those men if I can find them.'

Zarina did not answer. She shut her eyes and laid her head against his shoulder. 'Let us get out of this place,' Rolfe said. 'Can you walk, or would you like me to carry you?'

'I..I am..all..right,' Zarina answered with an effort.

Rolfe threw the axe down on the ground and put his arm round her. Picking up the lantern with his other hand they moved slowly. Walking through vault after vault, they reached the opening to the cellar. There was sunlight coming into the corridor through one of the windows. Zarina wiped the remaining tears away from her cheeks.

'What you need is a drink,' Rolfe said as he glanced at the cases of wine.

'I..I promised to..see Mrs Blossom,' Zarina said, 'and..really..I would..rather have a..cup of tea.'

'Very well,' Rolfe replied. 'I know you do not want anyone to know what has happened.'

'No..no..of course not,' Zarina said, 'but..those men will..come back..they may hurt..you.'

'I will take good care that they cannot get into the Priory again,' Rolfe said. 'Now come to the Kitchen, and leave me to make some arrangements before I take you home.'

'H..has Mr Bennett gone?' Zarina enquired.

'He left when he finished paying the bills,' Rolfe said. 'He thought you were staying on with me. I told him I would take you home. It was only after he had gone that I could not find you.'

'I thought you..would not..look in..the cellar.'

'I might not have done if Yates had not told me he had seen two men coming out of them. He thought perhaps they were stealing the wine, but when I looked there was nothing missing.' He smiled at her before he continued: 'Then by sheer good luck, I decided to see what was in the rest of the cellars.'

'It must have..been my..Guardian Angel telling you what..to do,' Zarina replied. She thought actually it was God and her father who had directed Rolfe how to find her. She was however too shy to say so to him.

They walked into the Kitchen where Mrs Blossom was waiting. 'Oi thought you'd forgotten us, Miss Zarina,' she said. 'Mr Yates told me as you'd be comin' an' Oi've bin waitin' for you.'

'You must have known I would not leave without seeing you,' Zarina smiled.

'What Miss Zarina would like,' Rolfe said, 'is a cup of tea with a lot of sugar in it. She has been exhausting herself looking round the Priory and it was you, Mrs Blossom who always said there was nothing like a nice cup of tea.'

'Indeed there's not!' Mrs Blossom said. 'An' if that's wot Miss Zarina wants, she shall 'ave it at once, as Oi'm just, so it 'appens, makin' a cup for meself.'

The tea-pot was standing on the stove. As Rolfe hurried away Mrs Blossom poured the strong Ceylon tea into two large cups. 'Ye're lookin' a bit pasty, Miss Zarina,' she said as she did so, 'so instead o' sugar, Oi'll put a spoonful o' honey in your tea. There be nothin' like honey for a "pick-me-up".'

'That is just what I need,' Zarina agreed.

She drank the tea and felt better. She sat chatting to Mrs Blossom and hearing all the local gossip until Rolfe returned. As he came into the Kitchen, Mrs Blossom said: 'Be it true, M'Lord, that as Mr Yates tells me, you an' Miss Zarina be engaged t'be married?'

'We are, Mrs Blossom,' Rolfe replied, 'and I am taking Miss Zarina away tomorrow to meet some of my relatives

113

in France. They will be hurt if they do not meet her before the announcement appears in the newspapers.'

'That'll be nice for you both,' Mrs Blossom said, 'an' when you comes back we'll 'ave th' Priory lookin' as it was when 'Er Ladyship were alive.'

'I am sure you will do that for me,' Rolfe said quietly. He led Zarina out of the Kitchen and through the back door towards the stables. He had apparently already given orders. One of his horses and *Kingfisher* were waiting for them. They set off across the Park.

Zarina glanced down the drive as if she expected to see Alf and Bill. They would return, snatch her cheque and get to London as fast as they could to cash it.

'How are you going to..prevent those men from..getting into..the house again?' she asked Rolfe.

'I have warned Yates that I fully expect the riff-raff to whom Darcy owed money to try to steal what they have not been able to buy. Yates and some of the other men are going to fasten all the shutters over the windows and bolt the door.' She was listening as he went on: 'Two stable-lads have offered to be on guard and are delighted to earn the extra money I have promised them.'

'That is very sensible of you,' Zarina replied, 'but, please..be very careful of.. yourself. And remember, you are picking me up very early tomorrow morning.'

'I have not forgotten,' Rolfe said.

They were riding under the trees and after a moment Zarina said: 'You know, I have no passport.'

'I will add you to mine,' Rolfe said briefly.

She knew it annoyed him to think she had to pretend to be his wife. Therefore she said quickly: 'It will be very exciting to go to India. It is a country I have always longed to visit.'

'I think by the time we get there you will only be too delighted to return to England,' Rolfe said rather coldly, 'and to the comfort to which you are accustomed.'

Zarina realised that once again he was resenting her money. He was determined he would not spend any of it on himself. She thought it would be a mistake to argue about it and instead she said: 'In a few minutes we shall reach flat land and I want to gallop *Kingfisher*. Are you prepared to race?'

'I will certainly try to beat you,' Rolfe replied.

'I shall be extremely annoyed if you do!' Zarina flashed.

They raced each other for nearly a mile. Zarina knew it was only by exceptionally good riding that Rolfe's horse was able to beat *Kingfisher* by a head. As they drew in their horses she said: 'Now I feel better.'

'I suggest you go home and have some sleep,' Rolfe said. 'You have come through a very unpleasant experience and I do not want you fainting on my hands tomorrow.'

'I will not do that, nor will I over-sleep,' Zarina promised. 'What I do not want is a row with my Uncle.'

'You should avoid that at all costs,' Rolfe agreed.

'I think, in fact, he will expect me to

be rather quiet and docile,' Zarina said reflectively.

'Then that is what you must appear to be,' Rolfe replied. To her surprise he suddenly pulled his horse up to a standstill. 'You are quite certain you are doing the right thing?' he asked. 'Perhaps if you put it to him sensibly how much you dislike the Duke he would agree to drop the idea and allow you to look around for someone more suitable.'

'No one could be more suitable to Uncle Alexander than the Duke of Malnesbury,' Zarina said, 'and if you do not take me away, Rolfe, I know he will somehow contrive to get me married and then I shall be lost for ever.'

There was a note of terror in her voice which Rolfe did not miss. 'Very well,' he said, 'I will pick you up at a quarter to five. Do not be late because if we miss the train we may also then miss the ship.'

'I will be there,' Zarina promised, 'and thank you.' She paused before she added: 'I think it would be a mistake for you to come in now and see Uncle Alexander. I am only praying that no one has yet told him that I announced our engagement at the Sale.'

'I should think it will remain a secret until tomorrow morning,' Rolfe said, 'then the servants will certainly be talking about it.'

'That is what I was thinking,' Zarina answered. 'Goodbye, Rolfe, and thank you again.'

'There is a lot of gratitude I want to express to you,' he replied.

'Keep it for the voyage,' she replied and rode off.

As she reached the stable-yard Jenkins came out. 'Oh, there ye be, Miss Zarina,' he exclaimed with obvious relief. 'Oi thought yer'd got lost.'

'I have been a long way,' Zarina explained.

'Oi thought as that's wot ye'd do first day back,' Jenkins remarked. 'An' 'ow did ye find the place?'

'Perfect!' Zarina smiled. 'Just as I expected. And *Kingfisher* was magnificent. You have kept him in very good trim.'

'That's just wot Oi 'oped ye'd say,' Jenkins replied. 'Will ye be ridin' again tomorrow?'

'I will let you know,' Zarina said evasively. 'Thank you, Jenkins. Goodnight!'

Jenkins led *Kingfisher* into his stall as Zarina walked towards the house. Suddenly she felt she could not face her Uncle at dinner, which was in about half an hour's time. She walked through the corridors to the hall and found Duncan there as she expected. 'I have been for a long ride, Duncan,' she said, 'and feel very tired. Will you tell the General that I have gone to bed? I would like something brought up on a tray.'

'Very good, Miss Zarina,' Duncan replied, 'and the General b'aint being alone.'

'Not alone?' Zarina questioned.

'No, Miss. He's asked th' Vicar and his wife t'dinner.'

'Quite a party!' Zarina exclaimed. 'Well, make my apologies. It has been a long day.'

119

'I'm sure they'll understand, Miss,' Duncan replied.

Zarina hurried upstairs, anxious to avoid her Uncle before she reached her bedroom. She was well aware why the Vicar had been asked to dinner. It was so that her Uncle could discuss with him the arrangements for the Wedding. Because it was her home and her Estate those she employed would expect a marquee in which they could toast her health in beer and cider. Doubtless they would also hope for fireworks in the evening, after she had gone away on her honeymoon.

It would all take a great deal of planning. The General, she knew, would enjoy that. She was certain he was already making out a list of guests. They would of course be received in the Ball-Room, and would undoubtedly amount to five hundred or more.

It was a wedding which Zarina had often thought of herself, when so many men were proposing to her, but that the Bridegroom should be an old man,—Duke or no Duke—was somehow not only horrifying but unpleasant. Once again, she was shuddering. She was afraid that after all she had arranged with Rolfe, her Uncle would somehow prevent her from getting away. She genuinely wanted to rest after her uncomfortable experience in the cellar. She knew, however, she had to have everything packed.

She let her Lady's-Maid undress her and she got into bed then she ate an excellent dinner that was brought up to her on a tray. When it was finished she said she wanted to go to sleep. Waiting until she was sure there would be nobody outside her bedroom door, she made her way to the attics. It was where the luggage was always stored. However, if she had to carry it herself in the morning, she would have to have something light. A heavy trunk would require the help of a footman.

There was an enormous amount of luggage which had accumulated over the years. At last she found two lightweight cases which had doubtless once belonged to a servant. They in no way compared with the real leather cases which her mother had used. Nor did they compare with those she herself had bought in London.

She took the two cases down to her bedroom and locked the door before she started to pack. She told herself she could take only the plainest things if Rolfe was right and they were travelling on a Cargo-Ship. Unfortunately, however, the gowns her Aunt had helped her to buy in London were all elaborate and very smart. She chose the plainest one in which to travel. She removed the trimming from the hat which went with her gown, hoping this would make her as inconspicuous as possible.

Having finished her packing she wrote to her Uncle, telling him that she was going to France. It was only then she remembered that she would need some money. It was all very well for Rolfe to say he would not allow her to pay for anything. She had the feeling when they got to India that he would abandon her. Then there would be no reason why she should not come home in the most comfortable P &

O ship available. She would then need the clothes which she was now forced to leave behind.

'I must have some money,' she thought and wondered how she could get some. She had a certain amount of jewellery of her own that she could take with her. Besides, of course, having her own cheque-book despite the fact that there had been an argument because her Uncle said his own Secretary could pay all her bills in London and Mr Bennett had the Power of Attorney. Zarina however, had wanted to be independent. Now she was glad she had won what had been a long tussle.

'I must have some cash,' she thought. She then remembered that Mr Bennett always kept a large amount in the safe to pay the wages on Fridays. Today was Thursday. He would therefore have the money ready in its neat little piles for tomorrow.

Wearing her dressing-gown and slippers she went down the stairs, hoping nobody would see her. Fortunately her Uncle was still in the Dining-Room. He would doubtless be talking to the Vicar even more volubly about the wedding now that his wife had left them to their port. She would be in the Drawing-Room and Zarina therefore avoided the main staircase.

It was easy for Zarina to slip into Mr Bennett's room without anybody being aware of it. She had known ever since she was in her teens where the key of the safe was kept. Often, after a large dinner-party, her mother would send her down to the safe with her jewellery. It was just a precaution in case someone burgled the house while they were out riding.

In those days Mr Bennett would be out supervising something at the far end of the Estate. He would, therefore not come to his office until late in the afternoon, or perhaps the next day.

It did not take Zarina long to find the key where he had always kept it and to open the safe. She had not been mistaken. There were little piles of money and also a number of notes. She helped herself to two hundred pounds, putting a note in their place to say what she had taken. Then she locked the safe and returned the key to the drawer.

She managed to get back to her bedroom without being seen, and got into bed. She felt she had been practical and very sensible. Her father would have commended her for the way by which she was trying to think out everything for herself. It would be fatal to make a mistake.

'I wish you were coming with me, Papa,' she thought after she had said her prayers. 'You always promised to take me abroad.' She smiled to herself. 'Now I have to go with Rolfe, who does not want me and who will doubtless make excuses not to show me India when we get there.'

Then she told herself that nothing mattered except that she would be free of her Uncle and the Duke.

Before she settled down to sleep she set the alarm on her clock. It was a new model she had bought in Bond Street for herself. She liked to go riding early in the morning and her maid was sometimes late in calling her. Now she was very grateful to have it. She set the alarm to go off at a quarter past four.

As she was exhausted she blew out the candles and lay down to sleep. Her last thought was that she might still be in the cellars at the Priory, or perhaps have met a brutal and nasty death.

'But I am alive! I am alive!' she found herself saying. It was a paean of delight. Then she added: 'And unless I am very unlucky, Uncle Alexander will not catch me!'

Chapter Five

When Zarina was dressed she cautiously opened her bedroom door. Everything was quiet and still, and the rising sun was already beginning to peep between the curtains. Having made certain there was no one about, she put the letter she had written to her Uncle on the table outside her door. She picked up her two cases and crept towards the back stairs.

There was no one to see or hear her as she went out through the door which led to the stables. As she expected, it was still too early for any of the young grooms to be moving about. Jenkins, she knew, would not come from his cottage for at least another hour.

She started to walk over the cobbled yard, finding the cases very heavy. It was a relief when Rolfe came towards her and took them from her hands. They did not speak because, as Zarina knew, voices carry at that time of day, as well as at night.

They walked quickly until she saw where Rolfe had parked his Chaise. Drawn by two horses it was out of sight of anyone who might be in the yard. He helped her into it, put the cases in the front beside the groom, and they drove off.

Only as they reached the gate in the meadow which led out onto the road did Zarina say in triumph: 'We have..done it! We have done..it!'

'I expected you would still be asleep,' Rolfe remarked.

She looked at him indignantly, then realised he was teasing her. 'I had so much to do that I only had about two hours' sleep,' she said. 'Then I was afraid I would not wake up and you would go without me.'

'I was wondering what I should do if you did not appear,' Rolfe said.

'I am quite certain you would have abandoned me to my fate!' Zarina retorted.

'Perhaps, and perhaps not,' Rolfe replied enigmatically.

Zarina, however, was thinking of the Priory when she asked: 'Did anything happen last night?'

'Not that I was aware of,' Rolfe replied. 'I gave Yates a mass of orders which I hope he will remember this morning, and then went to sleep.'

It was only a short distance to the Halt which was clearly marked 'Linwood Priory'. There was no Porter. Rolfe carried Zarina's cases onto the platform, then his own.

The Milk Train arrived on time. It was the sort of train Zarina had never been in before. She found it very different from the First Class Reserved Carriages in which she had travelled previously. Before they had died she had been in trains with her mother and father, and more recently with her Uncle. The seats in the Milk Train were of hard wood with no padding. There were no blinds or curtains over the windows. The Guard expected them to put their own luggage in his Van.

However, nothing mattered but that she was getting away. She had actually escaped without having to explain to her Uncle what she was doing.

When they reached London Rolfe found a Hackney Carriage which would take them to Tilbury Docks.

Zarina thought, when they arrived at the Quay, that it was an expensive ride, but she did not dare to offer to pay her share for fear of upsetting Rolfe.

They had to walk some way with all the luggage until they saw the Cargo-Ship in which he intended to travel. It was certainly not a very prepossessing vessel. It needed painting and Zarina could only hope it would not be as dirty inside as outside.

They walked up the gang-plank. The ship was being loaded with a strange collection of objects. One of them was a smart Chaise which Zarina guessed was being taken to India for some Officer of the Raj. It certainly would impress the peasants.

Having reached the decks Rolfe led the way inside. There appeared to be no one about. They went to where there was a glass window which obviously opened into an office.

'Is anybody there?' Rolfe called.

There was no reply.

Then a tall man in his shirt-sleeves with thinning red hair came to the window. 'I am Rolfe Wood,' Rolfe said, 'I have a cabin booked in my name. Are you the Captain?'

'I am,' the man replied, 'an' your cabin's ready for ye.' As he spoke with a strong

Scottish accent he looked questioningly at Zarina.

'Unexpectedly,' Rolfe said, 'I have brought my wife with me. We would like two cabins, if that is possible.'

'Your wife?' the Captain asked. 'Did ye say your wife?'

'Yes, my wife—Mrs Wood,' Rolfe answered.

The Captain looked Zarina up and down in a way she thought impertinent. Then he said somewhat surlily: 'Ah'm tryin' tae understand why ye want two cabins if you're married.'

'My husband snores,' Zarina said quickly, 'and it keeps me awake.'

The Captain looked at her suspiciously. Then he turned and went back inside the cabin which was hidden from them by a wooden panel.

Zarina looked at Rolfe a little nervously. 'What is he doing?' she asked in a whisper.

'He is looking to see if there is a cabin available for you,' he replied.

It never occurred to Zarina that there might not be a spare one. She waited anxiously for the Captain to re-appear. She was in fact, so nervous that she took off her gloves, feeling hot although it was still early in the morning.

The Captain came back. 'I have two cabins together,' he said, 'which I suppose is what ye want.'

'Yes, of course,' Rolfe said. 'Thank you very much.'

'But I still...' Suddenly he stopped. 'Now, where's yer weddin'-ring?' he asked in a different tone of voice. He was staring at Zarina's left hand.

For a moment she could only hold her breath. Then as Rolfe did not speak she answered: 'We..we had to..pawn it..to pay for the..voyage.'

'It seems tae me,' the Captain remarked, 'a bit strange, considerin' you're dressed up fine enough for Buckingham Palace.'

Zarina was well aware that although she had dressed as simply as she could she still looked out of place in this rough ship. Without really considering, but anxious to placate the Captain, she said: 'M..my gown..was a..present.'

'Tha's what I thought it might be,' the Captain said in a mocking tone.

Zarina did not understand, but Rolfe did and he said: 'I will thank you, Captain, not to insult my wife.'

The eyes of the two men met and for a moment there was silence. Then the Captain said slowly: 'I'm a God-fearin' man, and I'm havin' no hanky-panky on my ship. If you're married as you say ye are, Mr Wood, show me your Marriage Certificate, or else find another ship to tak' ye to India.'

Zarina looked up at Rolfe frantically. If they were delayed long her Uncle might discover where she was and prevent her from leaving England.

'I think you are being unnecessarily suspicious, Captain,' Rolfe was saying in a quiet, dignified voice. 'Allow me to show you my passport, on which is also written my wife's name.'

He drew the passport from his inside coat pocket. It had been issued by the Secretary of State for the Colonies and signed by the Earl of Kimberley (in very elegant longhand) and it stated that Rolfe Wood was a British subject.

As he put it down in front of the Captain Zarina could see that beneath the Earl's signature had been added:

'AND HIS WIFE, ZARINA WOOD.'

The Captain picked the passport up and studied it carefully, reading it from top to bottom. When he reached Zarina's name he said accusingly: 'This has been added!'

'Naturally,' Rolfe replied, 'I had the passport before I was married, and only arranged after the ceremony for my wife to be included so that she could travel with me.'

'I would still like tae see a Marriage Certificate!' the Captain said obstinately.

Again Zarina wondered frantically what they could do. Then, almost as if she was being guided by her father, she said: 'I am afraid I left it behind for the simple reason that I was afraid of losing it. But, of course, if you want to make certain we are legally man and wife, you can marry us yourself as soon as we are at sea.' She remembered reading in a book that the Captain of a ship had the power to marry his passengers if it was necessary.

The Captain looked surprised, but he said: 'Ye are quite right aboot that. Verra weel. Ye can have your two cabins, but as I have no wish for my other passengers to get the wrong impression, I think ye should wear a weddin'-ring.'

Neither Zarina nor Rolfe could answer him. They were so relieved at having won an unexpected battle.

The Captain handed through the window a piece of paper on which was written the numbers of the two cabins. He left them to find their own way to them.

With Rolfe carrying Zarina's luggage they went down the companionway and along a narrow passage. They looked at the numbers on the doors. Finally they found the two they required and went inside them.

The cabins were both small and narrow. Each contained two bunks, one above the other. There was, however, hardly room to turn round. Zarina was glad that she did not have to share her cabin with anyone, least of all a man as large as Rolfe. Neither of the cabins was particularly comfortable.

While they were deciding which one Zarina would have, a Steward appeared. He was as rough-looking as his Captain. He informed them that if they wanted sheets or blankets it would cost them extra, also the pillows. It seemed strange to Zarina. It was, however, obvious that Rolfe, having encountered this before, accepted the extra charge.

It was a relief when the bedclothes were brought to find that they were at least clean, although the blankets were well worn. Rolfe realised that Zarina was looking at them disparagingly and said: 'You will not need them for long. It will be very hot once we are in the Mediterranean, and hotter still when we reach the Red Sea.'

'I am not complaining,' Zarina answered, 'I am only trying to understand what happens in a ship like this.'

She spoke as tactfully as she could, but Rolfe said sharply: 'It is the best I can afford, and if you are not comfortable you have no one to blame but yourself.'

As he spoke he walked out of the cabin she had chosen for herself. He went to his own, slamming the door behind him. Zarina sighed. She knew he was resenting her presence. Also, she thought, he was determined to make it quite clear that he paid for himself and for her, even though it was something he could not afford.

'People with that sort of pride are foolish!' she told herself. She wondered how she could prevent him from being disagreeable about her money all the way to India. She also had the uncomfortable feeling that Rolfe would have to pay not only for an extra cabin. Because cabins should each have contained two people, he would have to pay for that too.

Then she told herself there was no use worrying about money at the moment. The only thing that mattered was that her Uncle would be reading her letter and would believe that she had gone to France. He would be furiously angry, but there would be nothing he could do about it. It could be two months before she need return and tell him that her engagement to Rolfe was ended.

Then she asked herself if that was long enough. Supposing she went back too soon? She might find the Duke had not given up the chase. But she was certain Rolfe would not want to keep her with him in India for long.

She walked to the porthole and looked at the river shimmering in the sunshine. 'Why am I worrying about the future?' she asked. 'What I have to do at the moment is to make Rolfe accept me without being disagreeable, and when I reach India, stay for as long as he will permit me to do so.'

She started to unpack her clothes. As she took them out of the cases she was sure that the Captain would disapprove of them. She could hear the sounds of the other passengers coming aboard.

When they were out of harbour they were

told there was a bowl of soup available at eleven o'clock. It was then that Zarina had her first sight of the other travellers.

The soup, which was thin and not particularly appetising, was being wolfed down by a motley collection of Asians. Also, there were three or four Englishmen who looked as if they were Commerical Travellers. There was only one other woman besides Zarina. She was an Indian, carrying a small baby in her arms.

When Zarina and Rolfe appeared, the other passengers stared at them in a way that was embarrassing. Two of the Englishmen nudged each other in the ribs. One of them said something about Zarina which made them both laugh. She and Rolfe drank a little of the soup because they were both hungry, having had no breakfast.

'I am sorry, Zarina,' Rolfe said when they went back to his cabin. 'If I had had any sense, I would have asked Mrs Blossom to give us some sandwiches.' He looked a little shamefaced as he added: 'My only excuse is that I am not used to travelling with beautiful ladies like yourself.'

'I might have thought of it too,' Zarina admitted, 'except that the servants at home might have been suspicious that I was going on a picnic so early in the morning.'

'Well, we have no one to blame but ourselves,' Rolfe said. 'let us hope that what we have for luncheon will at least be edible.'

Zarina could not help thinking it was a long time to have to wait until midday when luncheon would be served. However, she was so glad to be leaving England that she was prepared to put up with anything. All that mattered was that she was free of the Duke.

Soon the ship was well out to sea, which was smooth. There was still half an hour to wait before the meal. They were in Rolfe's cabin and Zarina was sitting on the lower bunk while he occupied the only chair. They were talking about India. Rolfe was telling her about the Monasteries he had visited in the Far North on his last expedition. Zarina found everything he said fascinating.

Then, just as she was asking him a question about the Monks there came a knock on the door. 'Come in!' Rolfe called out. When the door opened they saw it was the Captain who stood there. He was looking very much smarter than he had when they had first arrived. He was wearing his uniform coat and also his cap with its gold braid and peak. He came into the cabin.

'I've come tae marry you,' he said abruptly.

'Surely this is not necessary?' Rolfe exclaimed. 'I have assured you that Mrs Wood and I are married. It is just that we did not bring the Certificate with us.'

''Twas your wife, Mr Wood,' the Captain replied, 'who suggested I should marry ye again and there's already been remarks amongst the passengers and the crew about Mrs Wood's looks an' the way she's dressed.'

Rolfe looked angry. Zarina was afraid he might say something to upset the Captain. They were still in sight of the coast. It flashed through her mind that it would be easy for the Captain to make an excuse to put into a Port as they went down the English Channel and leave them there.

'If that is what you want, Captain,' she said, 'then I am only too willing to marry my husband for the second time, if only to make certain that he cannot leave me!'

She smiled as she spoke and the Captain's eyes twinkled. 'Ye have guts, Mrs Wood,' he said, 'I'll say that for ye.' He shut the door and they realised he had a Prayer Book in his hand. 'Now, stand in front of me,' he said, 'and let me remind you that this Service is binding—as binding as if ye were in a Kirk.'

Zarina looked at Rolfe thinking he was about to refuse to go through with it. Because she was anxious about the consequences if he did, she slipped her hand into his.

For a moment he did not move, then his fingers closed over hers. With an effort he rose to his feet.

The Captain read the Service quickly, but well. His heavy Scottish accent seemed to make it more formidable and binding than if he had actually been a Minister. They repeated the vows after him. It was obvious to Zarina that he had married several couples before because he did not falter. Only when he came to the part about 'giving and exchanging of a ring' did he hesitate. It was then that Rolfe drew the signet-ring from the little finger of his left hand. Zarina had not noticed it before. She thought the Captain would think it strange that they should have pawned her wedding-ring when Rolfe had this one. When he saw the ring, however, the Captain carried straight on with the Service. Lastly he said: 'By the power vested in me by Her Majesty Queen Victoria and as the Captain of this vessel, I pronounce you man and wife. May God bless your union!'

There was silence for a moment. Then Rolfe said: 'Thank you, Captain.'

'We are very grateful,' Zarina said quickly.

'I hope that's what ye'll be saying in the years ahead,' the Captain answered. Then he turned and left the cabin.

Rolfe waited until there was no question of his being able to overhear before he remarked: 'Now we really are in a mess! Why on earth did you suggest that he should marry us?'

'Because I thought he might turn us off the ship,' Zarina answered.

Rolfe gave an exclamation which was one of exasperation and moved to the port-hole. As he stood with his back to her Zarina said: 'Anyway, who is going to know that this has ever happened, except us?'

'What do you mean?' Rolfe asked.

'The Captain knows us as "Mr and Mrs Wood" and no one is likely to connect two people travelling in this Cargo-Ship with the Earl and Countess of Linwood!'

Rolfe turned round. 'What are you suggesting?' he asked.

'I am saying that once we leave this ship we can forget that this ceremony has ever taken place.'

'Are you serious?' Rolfe enquired.

'Why not?' Zarina answered. 'I have no wish to be married and nor have you. We will just pretend it never happened. I see absolutely no reason why anyone should think it did.'

Rolfe did not speak and she went on: 'When we get to India I suppose nobody will be interested in what you are doing in the Monasteries of Nepal. When it is safe for me to go home—I will still be Zarina Bryden.'

'I am certain it is not going to be as easy as that,' Rolfe said. 'As the Captain said, the ceremony is legal and binding.'

'Oh, well, I suppose we can have it annulled, if you want to go to Court,' Zarina replied. 'I still think it is best just to forget and pretend to yourself that it never happened.'

'That sounds easy,' Rolfe said, 'but, personally I think it is going to be extremely difficult for either of us to lie to the world and anyone we might meet in the future.'

'Let us cross that bridge when we come to it,' Zarina said. 'Anyway, I have no wish to marry anyone—for years!' Rolfe did not speak and she went on: 'You are not likely to find a wife in the Monasteries and therefore the question will not arise so far as you are concerned, for perhaps a very long time. When it does, you must just forget me.'

Rolfe did not reply, he turned back again to look out through the port-hole. Zarina felt as if he was deliberately forcing himself not to say how angry he felt, and what a mockery the whole episode had been. As if she felt he almost accused her she said in a very small voice: 'I..I am sorry..very sorry..if I have..done something wrong..but I was so frightened of having to..go back to Uncle Alexander..and to be truthful..I did not think of it from..your point of..view.' Still Rolfe did not speak and after a moment she continued: 'Do try to forget it! When you are no longer..encumbered by me..you will find it easier to..think the whole thing..never happened.'

'I hope you are right,' Rolfe said. 'At the same time we have got ourselves into a worse mess than we were in before. I must have some air! I cannot think, cooped up in here.' He walked out of the cabin and slammed the door behind him.

Zarina put her hands up to her face. She could understand quite well that he was feeling trapped. 'But what else could I have done?' she asked herself. She was aware that the Captain was a very obstinate man. If they had refused to allow him to marry them he would not have let them continue their journey in his ship. He would undoubtedly have put them ashore.

But Rolfe was angry and now she felt like crying. It had been hard enough to make him agree to their engagement. She was sure that it had never crossed his mind, any more than it had crossed hers, that they might have to be married.

'Anyway, I have saved the Priory for him,' she told herself, 'and I have got away from Uncle Alexander, so it was not really a very big price to pay.' At the same time she knew that Rolfe did not think of it in the same way that she did.

He came back into the cabin half an hour later when the bell had been rung to tell the passengers that luncheon was ready. Hardly speaking, and with a grim expression on his face, he escorted Zarina to the centre of the ship.

The Dining-Saloon, apart from the cabins, was the only place available for the passengers to sit. It was circular with no port-holes and no daylight. There were two long tables at which the passengers sat. The Captain was at the top of one of them and the First-Mate the other.

The food was brought in by a number of dark youths. Zarina was to learn later they came from numerous different countries in the East. There were even some Chinamen amongst them. They set the food, which was already on the plates, down on the table. While there was plenty of it, it was not very appetising. Zarina was in fact, not certain what it was except that it appeared to be a stew of some sort. It was served with two vegetables, one being potatoes, which were large and rather hard. There were loaves of bread on the table from which they could help themselves. The butter tasted slightly rancid, but the cheese was edible. The bread was at least fresh as it had just come aboard. But it was to grow staler and less palatable every day the journey went on.

The drinks brought round consisted mostly of beer and some bottles of what was called 'lemonade'. Zarina thought it was unlikely it had ever seen a fresh lemon. Rolfe had warned her that it was dangerous to drink the water. 'You may find it will upset you,' he said, 'especially because the barrels in which it is stored are seldom cleaned, even when the ship is in Port.'

This was depressing news until they found out that they were able to have large cups of tea or coffee with every meal. The coffee was not of the finest quality. But it was certainly preferable, Zarina thought, to the dubious lemonade.

She was well aware from the first meal onwards that the other passengers were staring at them curiously. Rolfe chatted with some of the Englishmen. While they talked to him Zarina knew they were looking at her, and it made her feel shy. She had brushed back her hair with a knot at the back of her head, but she could not disguise the colour of it, nor the translucence of her skin. Nor could she pretend not to be aware that her gown screamed 'Bond Street'.

Only the Indian woman with the baby did not seem to be interested in her. When they were leaving the Dining Saloon after the meal, Zarina stopped beside her and said: 'What a lovely baby! Is it a boy or a girl?' She spoke in English, then realised the Indian woman did not understand her.

But her husband, who was sitting beside her said: 'A girl, *Mem-sahib,* only two weeks only.'

'Is she your first child?' Zarina enquired.

'Yes, indeed, *Mem-sahib,* next time son.'

Zarina laughed. 'All men think like that.'

'*Mem-sahib* understand,' the Indian smiled, 'but my wife happy with little girl.'

'Of course she is,' Zarina smiled. 'I wish you good luck.'

The Indian bowed and Zarina went to

join Rolfe, who was standing a little aside. She thought perhaps he was annoyed at her for talking to the other passengers, but he said: 'If you want to speak to the Indians, I shall have to teach you some *Bengali*, although a great number of them do speak English, and quite well.'

'I would love to learn *Bengali*,' Zarina replied, 'but perhaps you will not let me stay in India long enough to use it.'

'That is another bridge we will have to cross when we come to it,' Rolfe remarked. She thought he was being evasive but at the same time, he was speaking pleasantly.

'Will you take me out on deck?' she asked. 'I want to have a last glimpse of England before it is out of sight.'

'Of course,' Rolfe agreed.

The ship rolled a little and she slipped her hand through his arm. 'After all,' she said softly, 'whatever happens, this is an adventure, and something we will always remember.'

'An adventure!' he repeated. 'Yes, Zarina, you are right. But I hope it is also something we do not regret.'

Chapter Six

It was rough in the Bay of Biscay. Although Zarina was not sea-sick she was glad to stay in her cabin and not walk about. She could imagine nothing more terrible than if she should break a leg or an arm when there was no one to look after her in the ship.

Rolfe went up on the bridge and became, strangely enough, friendly with the Captain. He was an interesting man, Rolfe told Zarina, and although it was hard to believe, very proud of his ship.

'I suppose it is the only possession he has,' Zarina said.

'I am sure that is true,' Rolfe replied, 'and as he started out as a Cabin-Boy, it has been his life's ambition eventually to have a ship of his own.'

When they reached the Mediterranean the sun was shining and the sea was the blue of the Madonna's robe. In a way, to Zarina, as she had spent so many years in Italy with her Cousin Mildred, it was like coming home. She ran about the deck taking as much exercise as possible with so much deck cargo on board.

Also, to her joy, Rolfe began to teach her *Bengali*. He was astonished at how quickly she learned until she explained why she was good at languages.

'Cousin Mildred,' she said, 'sent me to a School which was patronised by all the Aristocratic families in Italy as well as from the surrounding countries!' She counted on her fingers as she went on: 'There were girls from France, Germany, Switzerland, Portugal and Spain. I thought it amusing to make friends with them and, at the same time, learn their languages while they were trying to learn English.'

Rolfe laughed. 'Then you are multi-lingual.'

'I am delighted to think I can add *Bengali* to the list,' Zarina replied.

'I wish I had thought to bring some books with me,' Rolfe said, 'but instead you will just have to put up with my conversation.'

'I am quite happy to do that,' Zarina answered, 'especially if you tell me stories of where you have been and what you have been collecting besides manuscripts.'

'How do you know I have collected anything else?' he enquired.

'I just feel you would not be contented with one thing,' she answered.

He was not certain whether it was a compliment or not, but he told her he had seen some precious stones being mined in Turkey and Southern Russia. He told her how he had watched the Archaeologists in Egypt opening the graves of the long-dead Pharaohs. He added that, although he had very little money, he had managed to have a collection of his own. He had always intended to take it to the Priory.

'Where are these things now?' Zarina asked.

'They are in India,' he replied. 'I left them with a Maharajah who is a friend of mine and who promised to take care of them until I could take them home.' There was silence until he said: 'I had no idea I would have to leave for England because my brother had died. As I was in Calcutta at the time I just got on the first ship that was available.'

'Well, we can collect your treasures now,' Zarina said. She wondered as she spoke if he had noticed the word 'we'. Was he already planning to be rid of her as soon as they reached India?

Rolfe did not speak for a moment, then he said: 'You must understand that it is going to be difficult when we arrive in India to explain how you got there without a Chaperone.'

'You are not using your imagination,' Zarina said scornfully. 'Of course in the ship that brought us to Calcutta there was a Clergyman and his wife who very kindly acted as my Chaperone.'

As if he could not help himself, Rolfe laughed. 'You have an answer for everything!' he said. 'Very well, we will pretend that the Indian with the baby was the wife of a clergyman and make sure it is impressive enough by saying he was a Bishop.'

When he left her to go on deck, Zarina thought that at least she could make him laugh. He certainly did not seem so resentful of her as he had been when the voyage first started. They could laugh over the food which seemed to get worse and worse: and also the peculiarities of the other passengers.

It was possible, if anyone was prepared to pay for it, to have liquor of any description. The Englishmen apparently could afford what Rolfe thought was a high price for whisky, gin and brandy. They certainly began to get very noisy every evening at dinner. Zarina always made certain that she was seated at one of the other tables from them, or else as far away as it was possible to be. She still did not like the way they looked at her and it was obvious they made jokes to each other about her.

When they reached Alexandria they put into Port to take on fresh supplies and more coal. Zarina was entranced by the shops near the harbour. It was an opportunity for her to buy three thin gowns which she thought she would need when they entered the Suez Canal. It was certainly already very hot in Egypt. Because she was so thin and not very tall she managed to buy three very attractive gowns which fitted her. Two of them were of muslin and one of cotton.

To her surprise, Rolfe insisted on giving her a *kaftan* which was beautifully embroidered. She thought it must have come from Morocco. She was worried that he could not afford it, but she did not like to insult him by saying so. She only thanked him profusely.

She had to admit when she put it on that it was very becoming. As its colour was the blue of her eyes it accentuated the whiteness of her skin and the fiery gold of her hair. She knew it would be a mistake to wear it while they were in the ship. She felt, however, that Rolfe might be disappointed. She therefore put in on when they were alone in one of their cabins.

While they were in Alexandria they bought some food to supplement the fare on board. This, also, Rolfe insisted on paying for. When they returned to the ship they carried fruit, cakes, biscuits and some delicious almond and honey sweetmeats.

When they set off down the Suez Canal it was quite obvious that the Englishmen had concentrated on what drink they could buy. They were noisier than ever. Although Rolfe and Zarina had only said 'good morning' and 'goodnight' to them previously, they now insisted on being more friendly. Zarina had the uncomfortable suspicion that they were really trying to meet her. She therefore let Rolfe do all the talking and merely listened attentively to him.

They reached the Red Sea.

One evening after Zarina and Rolfe had been up on deck they came down to find the Englishmen rowdier than usual. They were in fact singing with very drunken voices. Zarina slipped quickly down the companionway, anxious to avoid them.

In her cabin she undressed and lay

158

down on the bed. It was now too hot even to need a sheet over her diaphanous nightgown which was very prettily adorned with lace.

She was just falling asleep when she heard a footstep outside her cabin door. Then there was a knock. She thought it must be Rolfe and sat up wondering what he wanted. Then a thick voice said in a whisper: 'Let me in!—Let me in—you pretty—little—bird!' The words were slurred and it was obvious that whoever had spoken had been drinking a great deal.

Zarina lay down again, knowing she had locked the door as she always did. It was then that whoever was outside turned the handle. When he found the door would not open he began to push against it, as hard as he could. Zarina was frightened. She knew the ship was not only old, but also not very well constructed. She was afraid the lock might give way and enable the man outside to come in. He was pushing against it harder and harder. Then, as the lock still held, she thought he murmured something about getting a screwdriver. It was then she became really terrified.

Getting out of the bunk she put on the thin negligée she had brought with her and slipped her feet into her soft slippers. There was only the light of the stars coming through the port-hole. She reached the door to find that the lock was in fact, pulling away from the wood. With a screwdriver and a little more effort the man, if he returned, would get into her cabin.

She listened to be certain he was not ouside, then hurriedly unlocked the door. She moved quickly to Rolfe's cabin and was relieved to find when she turned the handle that it was unlocked.

Rolfe was there, lying on his bunk reading a newspaper by the light of a lantern that hung from the ceiling. He looked up in surprise when he saw her. 'Zarina!' he exclaimed. 'What is it? What is the matter?'

'Th..there is a..man trying..to break into my..c..cabin,' she answered.

'One of those drunken Englishmen, I

160

suppose,' Rolfe said.

'I..I am..frightened that the..lock on the door will not..keep him out.'

Rolfe could see from the fear in her eyes and by the way that she spoke, how frightened she was. 'Turn your back,' he said, 'and I will get up and deal with him.'

For a moment Zarina was surprised at his command. Then she realised that he was naked and the sheet only covered him to his waist. She blushed and quickly did as Rolfe had said.

Standing in front of the port-hole she looked up at the stars. She heard him getting out of the bunk and knew he was dressing himself. Then she said: 'It would be a..mistake for..there to be any..trouble. We still have a..long way to go before we..reach India.'

Rolfe was still. 'You are right,' he said. 'It is very sensible of you. You can turn round now.'

Zarina did so and saw that Rolfe had put on his shirt and trousers. Then he looked at her. Her hair was falling over her shoulders and the thin negligée did not completely disguise the curves of her body.

'There is always this sort of trouble,' he said, 'where a pretty woman is concerned.'

She thought he spoke scathingly and she said: 'I..I am sorry..I would not have..come to you..if I had..not been..so frightened.'

'Of course you were frightened,' Rolfe said, 'and looking like you do you have no right to be in a ship like this.'

She felt he was angry again because of money but there was nothing she could say. She only looked at him piteously. After a moment he said: 'There is no need for you to be upset, or for me to knock his head off as I would like to do. Get into my bunk and I will sleep on the one above.'

'B..but we..cannot do..that!' Zarina exclaimed.

'Why not?' Rolfe asked.

'Because..you would be..uncomfortable.'

He thought she had been going to say something different and he smiled. 'I have slept in some very strange and uncomfortable places in the past,' he said, 'including the caves of wild animals. On one occasion when there was nowhere else available, I slept in an ditch.'

Zarina laughed as he meant her to do. 'At least tonight will be..better than..that,' she said.

'The person who is in danger is you,' he said, 'for if the bunks are as badly made as the rest of the ship I may easily fall on your head.'

'Then I will sleep on the top bunk and you sleep on the lower,' Zarina offered.

'You will do nothing of the sort,' Rolfe said. 'Get into the lower bunk and shut your eyes while I take off my clothes and climb up above.'

'I am..sorry to be such a..nuisance,' Zarina answered.

'Are women ever anything else?' Rolfe replied. However he spoke lightly and was obviously not angry.

Strangely enough, Zarina slept peacefully for the rest of the night. When she woke in the morning, Rolfe was already dressed. 'Oh, you are up already!' Zarina exclaimed.

'I have been viewing the damage done next door,' Rolfe explained. 'Your ardent admirer managed to force his way in and, as he found the cabin empty, he was obviously disappointed.'

'Did he break the lock?' Zarina asked. Rolfe nodded. 'Then you must get it mended before tonight.' She thought as she spoke that, whether the lock was mended or not, she would be frightened of being alone. The intruder, whoever he was, might contrive to join her.

As if Rolfe was following her train of thought he said: 'I think it would be wiser to stay as we are. As I have already said, you should not be aboard a ship like this, and you should not have to meet the scum of London, who always behave badly when they are abroad.' He spoke scathingly, but Zarina thought it would be a mistake to quarrel with the Englishmen. The most important thing was not to be noticed and certainly not be talked about once they had left the ship.

'You are quite right,' she said hastily. 'If you do not mind me sleeping here, I shall be quite safe. We know the Captain will approve of us being together.'

Rolfe laughed. 'That is certainly an important consideration.'

As they steamed through the Red Sea Zarina walked round the deck early in the morning, and late at night. For the rest of the time it was easier to sit in one of the cabins.

Zarina had her lessons in *Bengali* and persuaded Rolfe to continue telling her of his adventures. 'What you should do is write a book,' she suggested. 'I am thrilled by everything you have told me and I am sure there are thousands of people who would feel the same.'

'It is certainly an idea,' Rolfe said slowly, 'but I wonder if anyone in England really cares about what is happening on the other side of the world?'

'They may not want to leave their comfortable homes,' Zarina said, 'but they want to travel in their minds and their dreams, and that is what you can let them do.'

'I will certainly think about it,' Rolfe

said, 'but I have other adventures to experience first, which of course I can add to my collection.'

Zarina's heart sank. He was still thinking of going to Nepal. Perhaps, too, he might even go on to Tibet; in which case, he would not want her.

What was more, she was quite sure he could not afford it.

'What can I do?' she asked herself. 'What can I do to make him think I am indispensable?' It was then she knew that, however, disagreeable he was, she wanted to be with him. She felt safe and also, there was something about talking to Rolfe, and listening to him, which was very exciting. She could not explain why. But it was different from how she had ever felt before with the men who had fêted her in London and asked her to marry them.

'I want to be with him, I want to stay with him,' she thought, 'I want to talk to him.'

When she went to bed it was a joy to know that he was so near. If she was frightened she had only to call out and he would answer.

In the daytime they went on talking about the book he would write. By the time they were nearing India, she began to believe that he was convinced that it was something he must do.

As the days passed Zarina began to wish that the ship would go slower and that they would never reach Calcutta. Rolfe was still uncertain what he was going to do when they arrived. She thought that, perhaps, as soon as they did so he would find somebody who was returning to England and would insist upon her going with them.

'It is too soon for Uncle Alexander to be convinced I will not marry the Duke. If I returned without Rolfe he will insist that our engagement is broken off,' Zarina thought. She was too nervous to seek Rolfe's assurance that this would not happen because he might say it was exactly what he wished to do. And she could not prevent him from leaving her.

Because it was the only thing she could

do, she prayed frantically that he would not leave her.

Rolfe had been up on deck exercising himself and now the sun was beginning to sink. It had been unbearably hot during the day, and Zarina had felt too limp to make the effort of accompanying him. 'I will stay here,' she said as he got up to go, 'but..do not be..too long.'

'Lock the door if you are nervous,' he advised.

Zarina laughed.

'I am sure they are not yet as drunk as that,' she replied.

Almost every evening the Englishmen had been unpleasantly noisy at dinner. She thought, although she was not certain, that they would not try to come into her cabin again.

Rolfe went on deck and walked as much as he could, then he had a few words with the Captain.

'There is not a breath of wind,' he said unnecessarily.

'That's true,' the Captain said, 'an' we're verra lucky not to have had a passenger or a member o' the crew go down wi' the fever which happens when there's no wind an' it's verra hot. At least, that's what I've always found. And, as you ken, there's no Doctor aboard.'

Rolfe had made this journey often enough in the past to know that what the Captain said was true. When it was unusually hot in the Red Sea, there was always the likelihood of people going down with one of the Eastern fevers which could be dangerous.

Rolfe did not linger on the bridge, thinking that Zarina would miss him. When he went back to the cabin he saw to his astonishment that she was sitting in the chair with a baby in her arms.

'I am glad you are back,' she said. 'I need your help.'

'What are you doing with that baby?' Rolfe asked. He recognised it as the child belonging to the Indian woman.

'The mother is ill and her father brought her to me as I am the only other woman on board.'

169

'What does he expect you to do?' Rolfe asked.

Zarina smiled at him. 'I have to find some way of feeding her,' she replied. 'Her mother is too ill, and, needless to say, they have not such a thing as a baby's bottle on board.'

'Then what do you suggest?' Rolfe asked.

'I got the Steward to bring me some powdered milk which is not very appetising. I want you to pour it into the glove that you will see there on the dressing-table.'

'A glove?' Rolfe questioned.

'I made a hole in one of the fingers. I only hope the baby will understand she has to suck it.'

'I think that is very ingenious of you!' Rolfe exclaimed.

'I remember my mother telling me that it was something she once had to do for an Arab baby when she was travelling with Papa,' Zarina explained.

Following her instructions Rolfe filled a finger of the glove carefully with a little of the milk. At first the baby did not seem to understand. Then as a little of the milk trickled through the hole that Zarina had made, she began to suck rather feebly. At least she was having some nourishment.

It took some time and when Zarina thought she had had enough she put a little honey on the baby's tongue. She sucked that more eagerly. Then she picked the child up and laid her down gently on her bunk.

'I can see we are becoming over-crowded in here,' Rolfe said. 'I am just wondering where you are going to sleep.'

'She can sleep with me,' Zarina replied. 'She is so small that she will not take up much room.'

'What is wrong with the mother?' Rolfe enquired.

'Her husband thinks she has a fever and is too weak to move.'

Rolfe looked worried. 'I hope that is not true,' he said. 'The Captain was just congratulating himself about not having any fever on board, despite the heat.'

'Well, do not mention it to him,' Zarina begged. 'I have a feeling the Indian man does not want anybody to know that his wife is ill.'

Since she had learnt a little *Bengali*, Zarina had spoken to the Indian woman and her husband when they met in the Saloon for meals. She had been delighted when the woman had seemed to understand what she was saying. She was even more pleased when she found she could translate her reply into English.

'I am getting better at *Bengali*,' she had said to Rolfe only two days before. Then she wondered if she would have much chance of using it once she reached India. If he sent her back to England, then all of her efforts at learning the language as quickly as possible would be wasted. Because she was frightened of his answer, she still had not asked him what he was planning.

That night the baby slept peacefully beside her in her bunk. The next morning the baby's father was profuse in his gratitude. *'Mem-sahib* very kind,' he said.

'How is your wife?' Zarina asked.

He shook his head. 'Bad, very bad!' he

said, 'but better not tell Captain—be angry if anyone ill.'

When he had gone Zarina said to Rolfe: 'Do you think I ought to go down to see the baby's mother? Perhaps there is something I can do to help her.'

'You will do nothing of the sort!' Rolfe replied instantly. 'You must promise me, Zarina, that you will not go near them. In fact, I shall be very angry if you do.'

'I feel, as the only other woman in the ship, that I ought to do something to try to help her,' Zarina argued.

'If it is the kind of fever I suspect it is,' Rolfe replied, 'there is nothing any of us can do until we reach Calcutta. You are already helping her by taking care of her child.'

The baby cried and seemed restless. Later in the day she refused to take the milk, however hard Zarina persevered. The only thing she seemed to want was to be held close and walked up and down so Zarina moved up and down the cabin which was very small and constraining.

She did not, however, dare to take the baby anywhere else in the ship in case the Captain should think it strange that she had the baby with her, and ask where its mother was.

The Indian man had repeated when he last visited them first thing in the morning that he did not want the Captain to know that his wife was ill.

'We will be in Calcutta tomorrow,' Rolfe said cheerfully. 'Then you will be able to take her to the Doctor.'

The Indian had nodded but Zarina had the idea that it was something he did not intend to do when they arrived.

Because the baby had to be walked up and down, Rolfe went up on deck, then on the bridge.

He came down later than usual, knowing Zarina would be making the baby comfortable on the bunk before they went into the Saloon for dinner. When he opened the door he thought at first that the cabin was empty. Then he was aware that Zarina was lying on the bunk holding the baby close in her arms. He went a little nearer, then he realised that the child was dead.

For one terrifying moment when he saw that Zarina's eyes were closed, he thought that she too was dead.

Chapter Seven

Zarina opened her eyes, thought she must be dreaming, and then closed them again. Then when she took a second look she found she was in a huge room, exquisitely furnished, with *punkahs* moving on the ceiling. She could see trees through a large window. She lay trying to think where she was. Then she was aware that there was an Indian woman by her side who was lifting her head so that she could drink. She was very thirsty and the drink, which was made of mangoes and limes, was delicious.

The Indian woman set her head down gently on the pillow and with an effort Zarina managed to ask: 'Wh..where..am ..I?'

'If you talk, *Mem-sahib,* you better, soon well,' the Indian woman replied. She hurried from the room and Zarina thought she had gone to fetch somebody.

'Where..am..I? What is..happening?' she asked herself. She tried to remember, but all she could think of was Rolfe. Where was he? Where had he gone and why was he not with her?

The Indian woman came back and now there was an elderly man with her. He came to the bedside and immediately felt for Zarina's pulse. She guessed he was a Doctor.

'How are you feeling?' he asked.

'How..how..long..have I..been..ill?' Zarina questioned.

'You have had what we call "Five-day Fever",' he answered.

'A..fever?' Zarina murmured.

'You had a very high temperature and were more or less unconscious,' the Doctor said. 'All you have to do now is to get better.'

'But..where am..I?' Zarina managed to ask.

'You are in Viceregal Lodge,' the Doctor answered, 'and I have been looking after you. May I say that I am very proud that my patient looks so beautiful, despite what she has been through.' He was so complimentary that Zarina managed to smile at him.

The doctor turned to speak to the Indian woman in *Bengali* but Zarina understood. He told the woman that his patient must be kept quiet, to be given as much food as she could eat, and plenty of drink. He finished by saying: 'In another twenty-four hours she will be on her feet again. This fever does not linger.'

As he spoke the Indian woman kept nodding her head and saying: 'Yes, *Sahib!* Yes, *Sahib!*' in obedience to everything he told her.

The Doctor then turned to Zarina. 'I want you to eat and drink as much as you can,' he said, 'and I will come back to see you this afternoon.'

He walked to the door, then looked back and smiled at her. 'You will soon be joining your husband downstairs.'

He was gone before Zarina could ask him when Rolfe was coming to see her.

The Indian woman had also left the room and she was alone. It felt as if her brain was full of cotton-wool and it was hard to think clearly. She could remember the ship, and of course the baby who she had tried to make drink, and Rolfe.

'I..want..him,' she murmured. Because she felt weak he would make her strong again.

When the Indian woman came back she was carrying a tray. It contained food and she set it down beside the bed. Zarina thought she was not hungry, but when she tasted the dishes the woman had brought her, she found she wanted to eat. Everything she tasted was delicious and easy to eat with a spoon.

By the time she had finished, she felt much stronger and she wanted to ask for Rolfe. Then she remembered that, if he said they were just engaged as they had planned to say when they left England, it would be considered improper for him to come to her bedroom.

'I must..see..him,' she thought desperately. 'I..must!'

Then she recollected, and at first it had not registered with her, that the Doctor had said 'your husband'. Had Rolfe really said that they were married? Slowly her mind went back to the time when they had been married in the ship. She had told him that when they reached India they could forget all about it. As she went on thinking it over, she decided because she was ill, he had been forced to stay on at Viceregal Lodge. He had intended going there only to pick up his letters. Now he had been obliged to say that they were man and wife.

'It will..make him..very..angry,' she thought and felt herself shiver.

She had been certain that the strange marriage which had taken place because the Captain had said he was a 'God-fearing man' could easily be forgotten. Now Rolfe had announced she was his wife and they were in Viceregal Lodge of all places!

'I do..not..understand,' she muttered.

It was upsetting to think, because she

had been ill, that all their plans had gone awry. Now it would be very difficult for Rolfe to be free. She was sure he would be furious with her for having in a way trapped him.

The Indian woman, having cleared away the tray, came back to lower the sun-blinds. Then she said: *'Mem-sahib* have bath, feel better.'

'I would like that,' Zarina agreed.

A bath was brought into the room by several other women and set down on the floor. Water was poured into it.

When Zarina had washed as comfortably as she was able to do at home, she was wrapped in a big Turkish towel. It could only have come from England. The water had been scented with almond-blossom and two Indian women helped her to dry herself. They brought her one of her own nightgowns and, having put it on, she got back into bed.

The sheets and pillow-cases had been changed while she was having her bath, which had, although she had enjoyed every moment of it, been somewhat exhausting.

As soon as she was safely back in bed Zarina shut her eyes.

She had not intended to go to sleep, but she must have slept for several hours. When she awoke she was aware that, despite the *punkahs*, the air was much hotter.

When she saw that she was awake the Indian woman hurried to fetch her more food. This time, Zarina realised it was luncheon. As she sampled the delicate dishes that were provided for her she could not help thinking how different they were from the food she had eaten on board the ship.

There was still no sign of Rolfe. She was still afraid to ask for him in case she said the wrong thing.

The Indian woman took away the tray, then drew the sun-blinds a little lower. '*Mem-sahib* sleep,' she said. 'Now everyone rest.'

Zarina knew she was saying it was *Siesta* time. Rolfe had told her, although she had known it already, that everything in Indian stopped after luncheon. In the blazing heat of the day, even the Indians put up their feet and rested.

But as she had just been asleep, she did not feel tired. When the Indian woman had left her, she lay looking round at her luxurious bedroom. She was thinking how different it was from the cramped cabins and the rough bunks. The bed in which she was now lying was very large. It had a golden Corolla attached to the ceiling from which fell white frilled muslin curtains. They were caught up at each side with golden Cupids.

'The emblem of Love,' she thought.

The door opened. As she wondered why the Indian woman had come back, she saw with a leap of her heart that it was Rolfe. She gave a cry of joy and sat up a little.

'Oh, Rolfe!' she exclaimed. 'I have been..longing to..see you!' The words seemed to tumble out of her mouth without her thinking.

He came nearer to her. As he did so she saw that he had undressed obviously ready for the *Siesta*. He was wearing a thin

182

white linen robe. He looked, she thought, extremely handsome; in fact, even more handsome somehow than she remembered.

He reached the bed and, looking down at her, said: 'I hear you are better. In fact, the Doctor tells me you will soon be well.'

'How could I have caught a fever and upset..everything?' Zarina asked apologetically. 'I am..sorry for being..such a nuisance.'

'You caught it from the baby,' Rolfe explained, 'or rather from her mother.'

'The baby!' Zarina exclaimed. 'Is she all right?'

Rolfe reached out his hand to take hers. 'She died,' he said quietly.

'Oh..no!' Zarina exclaimed. 'Poor little thing..I tried so..hard to keep her..alive!'

'I know you did,' Rolfe answered sympathetically. He saw the tears were running down Zarina's cheeks and he said: 'For God's sake, darling, do not cry. I will give you a baby of your own.'

For a moment Zarina could only stare

at him and her eyes seemed to fill her whole face. Then she asked in a voice he could hardly hear: 'What..what did you..say to me?'

'I have so much to say to you,' Rolfe answered. 'First of all, my precious, I have to ask you to forgive me.'

Zarina felt as if the walls of the room were whirling round her. At the same time, her heart was whirling with them. 'I..I do not..understand,' she murmured.

'I have asked myself over and over again,' Rolfe said, 'how I could have been so cruel and so utterly and completely insensitive as to take you on board that ship.'

'W..what was..wrong?' Zarina asked.

'Everything was wrong,' he said, 'and it was appallingly wrong of me to imagine for a moment that you, looking like you do and being what you are, should be subjected to anything so appalling.'

'I..I was safe..with you.'

Rolfe smiled. Then he said: 'I did nothing the right way. If you only knew how much you made me suffer you would realise that "safe" is the last word you should use.' Zarina looked bewildered and he said: 'I will never again, my darling, go through the torture that I endured when you came to my cabin and slept beneath my bunk, then brought the baby in as well.'

'I..I was afraid the..baby would..upset you,' Zarina said.

'It was not the baby that was upsetting me, it was you!' Rolfe said. She looked at him in a puzzled fashion, still not comprehending, and he explained: 'I fell in love with you, my darling, before we had even left England, but I was determined you should not be aware of it and that, when you were safe from your Uncle and the Duke, I would go away and try to forget you.'

'I was..so afraid..that was..what you would..do,' Zarina murmured.

'It was what I was determined to do,' Rolfe said. 'Until, my sweet, I realised you loved me.'

Zarina's eyes met his and she blushed. She knew as he spoke, and from the way he had been speaking to her already, that what she had been feeling for him was Love. She wanted him, she felt she must be near him and had been terrified that he would leave her.

Of course it was Love!

It was Love, but she had not understood.

She had only been desperately worried in case he would be angry with her.

'How..how did you..know that I..loved you?' she asked in a very small voice.

'When I realised that you had the fever which is well known in this part of the world,' Rolfe said, 'there was nothing I could do on board the ship except try to keep your temperature down. I put cold cloths on your head and got the Captain to communicate with the Viceroy.'

'He must have been surprised to learn that you were so grand!' Zarina smiled.

'When he knew who I was,' Rolfe replied. 'I think he was very impressed. But the only thing that mattered was to get you somewhere where you would have proper attention.'

'So you brought me..here,' Zarina murmured, 'but..how did you..know I..loved you?'

'When the ship docked and we moved you on a stretcher from the bunk in my cabin,' Rolfe explained, 'you kept murmuring over and over again: 'Please God..do not..let him send me away..please, God, let me stay..with him..I love him..I love..him!' His voice was very deep as he repeated the words.

Zarina's eyes flittered and the colour rose in her cheeks. 'You..must have felt..embarrassed,' she whispered.

'I felt as if I could jump over the moon,' Rolfe replied. 'You had told me you had no wish to marry me, but I wanted you..I want you now, desperately, as I have never wanted a woman before!'

'Oh, Rolfe, is that..true?'

Zarina lifted up her arms and Rolfe pulled her against him. He kissed her gently, as if he was afraid to hurt her. To Zarina it was as if he carried her into the heart of the sun and a golden light enveloped them. She had never been kissed and it was a rapture. Rolfe's kisses were exactly what she had thought a kiss would be like, if she loved the man who gave it to her.

He kissed her at first very gently, then as he felt her lips quiver beneath his, his kiss became more possessive, more passionate. Finally he raised his head and in a voice that sounded unlike his own he said: 'It is time for *Siesta,* my darling, and I want to rest with you. After all, we *are* married!'

There was no need for Zarina to answer. He saw the radiance in her face and her eyes seemed to be filled with stars. He took off his robe and slipped into the bed beside her, pulling her close to him. 'I love you, my precious,' he said. 'I love you until I can think of nothing but you.'

'I..I thought you were..angry because I had forced my money..on you. Does..that not..matter?'

She could hardly say the words, but somehow she had to know the truth.

For a moment Rolfe did not reply and she said quickly: 'You can..give it..away..get rid of it..anything..so long

188

as..you go on..loving me.'

Rolfe laughed, and it was a very happy sound. 'It is typical of you to think like that,' he said. 'But we have the only thing that matters, my darling, and that is Love.'

Then he was kissing her again, kissing her until she felt as if it was impossible to know such rapture and not die from the wonder of it.

Unexpectedly, Rolfe released his hold on her and to her surprise, moved a little way from her. 'You have been ill, my darling,' he said. 'Now I think you should rest.'

The way he spoke sounded somehow strange and Zarina gave a little cry. 'I..I do not want to..rest,' she cried. 'I want to be with you. I want you to kiss me..Oh, Rolfe..do not stop..loving me!'

'I have not stopped,' he said, 'but I am afraid of upsetting you. I want you, my lovely one, I want you desperately, wildly, madly, if you like, but I am trying to think of you.'

'I..I want you,' Zarina whispered. 'Oh, please, Rolfe, go on loving me. It is so..wonderful that I..feel as if I am..in.. Heaven.'

Then he was kissing her again: kissing her until he carried her into a Heaven that was all their own.

The room became filled with the sunshine of their Love.

It seemed to burn through them both so that they were no longer human, but one with the Gods.

A long time later Zarina stirred against Rolfe's shoulder and he said: 'My darling, my precious—I have not hurt you?'

'I did not..know that love could be..so wonderful!' Zarina whispered. 'Oh, Rolfe, how can I ever have thought of..marrying anyone but you?'

'I was determined never to marry,' Rolfe answered, 'but it was because I did not know that anyone as perfect as you existed.'

'I am sure it was God, or perhaps Papa..that brought us together and solved all our problems!' Zarina said.

She was thinking how, just by chance,

she had gone home from London and found the Priory was being sold up the next day. She might so easily have missed it all by twenty-four hours. She would not have met Rolfe, who would have gone to India. Even to think of how nearly she had missed this incredible happiness made her tremble.

She put her hand on Rolfe as if to hold him closer to her as she said: 'I love you..I love you..and if we had to live together in a cave, I would be just as..happy as I am..now.'

'If you think I would ever take the chance of losing you again, you are very much mistaken!' Rolfe said. 'It was through my pig-headedness you became so ill, and I was afraid I might lose you.' His voice deepened as he said: 'It was only when I knew that, if you died, I had no wish to go on living.'

Zarina moved a little closer to him. 'That is how..I have always wanted..someone to..love me,' she said, 'because I was me.'

'No man could do anything else but

love you for yourself,' Rolfe replied. 'No one could be braver, or more intelligent than you. I realised, when we were in that rough ship, what an exceptional person you were.' He kissed her hair and went on: 'You never complained, even of the appalling food, the discomfort, and those very uncouth and unpleasant passengers.'

'I..I wish I could have..saved the..baby,' Zarina said. 'I did..try.'

'No one could have done more,' Rolfe answered. 'When I saw you holding that child in your arms, I wanted to go down on my knees and worship you.'

Zarina gave a little laugh. 'If that was what you thought, you were very deceitful,' she said, 'because I was so frightened that you were angry with me..and would leave me as soon as we reached India.'

'If you think you can escape from me you are mistaken!' Rolfe said. 'Incidentally, to make sure that you are mine I have sent an announcement of our marriage to *The Times* and to the *Morning Post.*' He smiled at her then went on: 'When your Uncle reads it he will know that he is no longer your Guardian, nor has he any jurisdiction over you.'

'Instead I have you,' Zarina said softly. Turning her head, she pressed her lips against Rolfe's shoulder.

There was a fire in his eyes as he pulled her closer to him. With an effort he said: 'I am sure, my darling, that I should let you rest.'

'I thought..that was what..we were..doing,' Zarina replied.

Rolfe laughed. 'Some people might think otherwise,' he said, 'but if this is your idea of resting, my precious one, then I am very, very happy to go on doing so.' Then he was kissing her again and Zarina felt as if they were flying towards the sun.

The heat was abating a little when Rolfe said: 'I suppose I ought to go down to inform the Viceroy that you are better. Of course you will not be able to meet him this evening, and therefore I will dine here with you in your bedroom.'

'Can you do that?' Zarina asked eagerly.

'It is what I intend to do,' Rolfe

answered. He kissed her tenderly before he got out of bed and put on his robe. 'Is there anything you want, my darling?' he asked.

'Only you,' Zarina answered. 'Oh, Rolfe, is it really possible that we can be so happy and still be alive?'

'I intend to make you even happier,' Rolfe answered. 'We will talk about that as soon as I explain to the Viceroy how much better you are and thank him for having you here in such comfort.'

'Of course you must do that,' Zarina agreed, 'and, incidentally, who is he?'

Rolfe smiled. 'I thought you would know that, but of course on our journey to India you did not expect to be staying at Viceregal Lodge.'

'Judging by the ship you had chosen,' Zarina replied, 'I expected a hovel in a back-street, or perhaps just a shelter made of bamboo!'

She was teasing him and Rolfe laughed. 'I had thought of something like that,' he said, 'but fortunately, the Earl of Dufferin is a distant Cousin of mine. There was no difficulty about us being welcomed here as his guests.'

'That certainly makes things easier,' Zarina answered. She was thinking as she spoke that they would not have to pay for their accommodation. The question of money would not therefore arise.

Rolfe walked towards the door. 'I will not be away long,' he promised. 'You know, my darling, I want to be with you, and I shall make that quite clear to our host.' He smiled at her as he opened the door.

When he had gone, Zarina lay back against the pillows thinking that what had happened could not be true. How could Rolfe love her? How was it possible that from being anxious, frightened and terrified at the thought of having to go back to England alone, she was in Paradise?

They were married, they were man and wife, and there was no question of them having to pretend otherwise.

'Oh, thank you, God, thank you!' she said. It was a prayer that came from the very depths of her heart.

She felt, too, that her father had somehow been directing her and making certain she would come to no harm. Only he could have made sure she found the one man in the world she could love and who would love her.

Perhaps in the future there would be difficulties, especially about her money, but because their love was so great it would not really be of any importance.

'I love him! I love him!' she murmured.

Then she fell asleep.

It had grown very much cooler.

Zarina had another bath, during which time the bed had been remade. Now she was waiting expectantly for Rolfe. She was wearing one of her pretty nightgowns and had arranged her hair. She thought she looked very much smarter than when he had first seen her after luncheon.

He did not come back as quickly as she had hoped, but he sent a message to say that the Viceroy wanted him and that he would come to her as soon as possible.

She had been asleep for a long time

when she got his message. Now the sun was sinking. She thought the room would be very romantic when the candles were lit.

The Viceroy must surely have finished with Rolfe by this time and he would come straight to her. She was not mistaken. The door opened and he came in, looking exceedingly smart in a white suit she had not seen him wear before. He was carrying a bouquet of flowers in his hand. He set it down in front of her and she saw that the flowers were all white. There were roses, orchids, stephanotis and lilies, mingled together to make what would have been a perfect bouquet for a Bride.

'Are these for me? How lovely!' she said.

'They are for my wife,' Rolfe replied, 'and the first present I have ever given her.'

'Thank you..thank you..very much!' Zarina smiled.

'I have another present for you,' Rolfe said, 'In fact, two.' He put two small jewel-boxes down in front of her as he spoke.

She looked at them for a minute before opening one, to find that it contained a wedding-ring. 'Oh, Rolfe..darling!' she exclaimed. 'I would rather have this than..anything else..in the..world!'

Rolfe took the ring out of the box. Then he kissed her hand before placing the ring on the third finger. 'Now you are bound to me for Eternity,' he said, 'and there is no escape.'

'I..I do not want..any,' she answered.

'Now look at your other present,' he said.

She opened the other jewel-box and gave a gasp. Inside there was also a ring. But this one was of a large diamond in the shape of a heart and it had smaller diamonds all round it.

'Oh..Rolfe..!' Zarina gasped. Then she said: 'It is lovely..perfectly..lovely..but how could you..?'

She stopped. She felt what she had been about to say would cause him embarrassment.

Rolfe finished the sentence for her. '..how could I afford it?' he asked. 'That is something I am going to tell you.'

She looked at him anxiously. It struck her that perhaps he had done something rash. Even though he was in India he must have sold something from the Priory so as to buy her what was obviously an expensive ring.

Rolfe sat down on the side of the bed and drew a letter from his pocket. 'I have just received this from Bennett,' he said.

'He has written to you?' Zarina asked. 'But, why..what has happened?' She felt, if it had not been disturbing, Mr Bennett would have written to her. Even though he might be explaining what was happening on the Priory Estate, he was still her employee.

'I will read it to you,' Rolfe said, 'and after I have done so, you can kiss me for giving you those presents.'

Zarina had not taken the diamond ring out of the box. She only looked at it, thinking how beautiful it was. At the same time, she was worried.

Rolfe took the letter out of its envelope and opened it. Slowly, as if he wanted to savour every word he read:

'*My Lord,*

I hope you receive this letter as soon as you arrive in India, in case I have done anything that is not completely to your liking.

Zarina made a little sound and put out her hand towards Rolfe. As he was holding the letter she laid it on his knee, feeling that to touch him was some comfort.

Rolfe continued.

'*As soon as Your Lordship and Miss Zarina had left I made a thorough investigation of the Priory to make sure that everything had been put back in its rightful place. I found a few things that needed repair, but otherwise nothing of importance to be done.*

I then visited the cellars, thinking perhaps I should replenish some of the wines that were necessary before Your Lordship's return...'

Rolfe paused as if to take several breaths and looked for a moment at Zarina who was watching him intently. Because she looked so lovely he could not help bending forward to let his lips rest for a moment on hers. Then, before she could speak, he went on:

'When I was investigating the empty cellars, I found at the far end some damage had been done to a vault that was very old. The door had been broken but attached to it was a cheap chain such as are used on carriages to secure trunks...'

Rolfe glanced at Zarina. He was thinking how he had found her tied up! How he had freed her with the axe. Then he read:

'When I told the Estate Carpenter from Linwood to repair the door, he discovered to my astonishment, and his, that the broken door was made of gold!'

Zarina gave a cry. 'D..did you say..gold?'

'Gold!' Rolfe confirmed. 'And Bennett goes on:

'In fact the whole of the front of the vault which appeared to be empty was made of solid gold and I hope Your Lordship will think I did the right thing.

Because I realised that it must have been done at the time of the Dissolution of the Monasteries, I called in experts from the British Museum to make a further inspection.

In the open sides of the vault, which appeared to be empty, they discovered that the treasure belonging to the Monks had been walled in.

This comprised two chalices made of gold and set with precious stones, a Cross and what appeared to be goblets and bowls which they think must have been used at the Abbot's table.

There were other things, such as bookmarks, and pendants, all of great value, not only historically, but also because the stones themselves are so fine.

The treasure in being moved into the

care of the British Museum to await Your Lordship's instructions, while the gold, of which there is a considerable amount, is in safe-keeping.

The British Museum considers the value of such treasure to be somewhere in the region of a million pounds sterling, although when it is finally collected and weighed, it may even be more.

I am only hoping, my Lord, that I have taken the necessary steps to preserve the Treasure in safety until Your Lordship's return...'

Rolfe finished reading the letter and looked at Zarina. 'I do not..believe..it! I just..do not..believe it!' she cried.

'I do,' Rolfe said. 'I am now a rich man, but darling, all the riches in the world are unimportant beside that fact that I own you!'

He bent forward as he spoke and took her in his arms. 'I love you!' he said. 'If they found that the whole Priory was made of diamonds and the fields had turned to gold, it would be quite unimportant beside the fact that you love me.'

'I do love you..I do love you..Rolfe!' Zarina said. 'Now I need..worry no more..about my..money.'

'We can forget it,' Rolfe said. 'Now I can give you all the things I want to give you and pay for them myself.'

He spoke with the elation of a small boy, and Zarina said: 'You have already given me the sun, the moon and the stars! And Rolfe, I love your..rings and I am so..happy that you have such a..marvellous treasure. But it cannot compare with your..kisses..and how I..feel when you.. make me..yours!'

She whispered the last words and because she was shy the colour rose in her cheeks.

Rolfe looked at her for a long moment before he said: 'I adore you! I worship you! You are right, my darling. We have everything that really matters. I am only glad that Bennett has found such a treasure because I can share it with you, and of course, leave it when we die, to our children.'

Zarina made a little movement and hid her face in his neck.

'You want a baby,' Rolfe said, 'and, darling, what could be a better place for our sons and daughters than the Priory and your estate, which can be incorporated with mine?' He pulled her a little closer before he said: 'I think we should go home and set our house in order. Would you like that?'

'Oh, Rolfe, can we do that? What about the Monastery you wanted to visit?'

'We will come back in future years,' Rolfe said, 'but now I want to take you home. You have to make the Priory as perfect as it was when my grandfather lived there and when the Monks had it in the first place.'

'We will do that..of course we will do that,' Zarina cried, 'and we will make everybody who works for us, as well as the villagers and the farmers, happy, as we are.' As she spoke, she put her arms round Rolfe's neck and drew his face down to hers.

Then he was kissing her; kissing her

wildly, passionately and at the same time, possessively.

He knew as he did so that he was right in thinking that nothing was really important beside the Love they had found together.

The Love that made them one person and which had come unexpectedly from God.

He knew better than anyone else what Mankind had sought and strived for all down the centuries.

It was—Love.

This Large Print Book for the Partially sighted, who cannot read normal print, is published under the auspices of

THE ULVERSCROFT FOUNDATION

THE ULVERSCROFT FOUNDATION

. . . we hope that you have enjoyed this Large Print Book. Please think for a moment about those people who have worse eyesight problems than you . . . and are unable to even read or enjoy Large Print, without great difficulty.

You can help them by sending a donation, large or small to:

**The Ulverscroft Foundation,
1, The Green, Bradgate Road,
Anstey, Leicestershire, LE7 7FU,
England.**

or request a copy of our brochure for more details.

The Foundation will use all your help to assist those people who are handicapped by various sight problems and need special attention.

Thank you very much for your help.